Sammy in Italy

Single Wide Female Travels
Book 2

By

Lillianna Blake

ISBN: 0692626263
ISBN-13: 978-0692626269

DEDICATION

To all women out there dreaming of
eating gelato in Italy! You must go to Italy! ☺

TABLE OF CONTENTS

CHAPTER 1

Memories of France swirled through my mind. With Max by my side, I'd made a few big strides, not the least of which was experiencing a topless beach. Now a brand new adventure awaited. Italy—and more specifically, Venice. I couldn't think of a more romantic place to spend time with Max.

When I looked over at him, his nostrils flared a bit in his sleep. I couldn't help but smile. He was cute, even while he slept. I slipped my hand from his and pulled a magazine out of my bag to look through. It featured Venice's latest trends.

It was hard to wrap my head around the idea that these were real women on the glossy pages. From flawless skin to perfect figures to deep soulful eyes—they looked more like goddesses than mere mortals. I shifted in my seat and flipped the page. It was important to me to have an idea of what women in Italy might think of as beautiful. To my surprise, I'd discovered in France that beauty could be quite different between countries. I wanted to be sure that I could speak clearly to my audience.

After some time, the conductor of the train announced our arrival at the Venice station. With a light touch I tapped Max's knee.

"Not on the train, sweetie." He brushed my hand away.

I raised an eyebrow and tapped his knee again.

"Alright, fine—if you insist." He shifted in his seat and attempted to kiss me.

"Max!" I laughed and snapped my fingers in front of his face to wake him.

He blinked a few times, then kissed me anyway. When he broke the kiss he smiled sleepily at me. "Sorry, I was having a wonderful dream."

"We've arrived in Venice." I pointed to the passengers who had begun to gather their belongings.

"Wow, I can't believe I slept through the whole trip. Did you?"

"Not a wink." I sighed. "I'm going to need coffee—and fast."

"Weren't you comfortable?" He gathered a few of our bags.

"I was. I guess I'm just too excited about Venice."

He took my hand and led me down the aisle and off the train. The station bustled with people headed in all directions. Max snagged a luggage cart and added a few of our bags to it. "That should be everything. Any idea where we're going next?"

"Yes." I reached into my pocket for the itinerary, which included a voucher to rent a car. To my horror, all I found was pocket lint. "Oh no." My eyes widened.

"What is it?" Max gripped the handle of the luggage cart.

"I must have left the itinerary on the train. I'll just run back and get it."

"Sammy, I don't think that's a good idea." He reached for my hand, but I pulled it away before he could grasp it.

I refused to start our first day in Venice like this. That itinerary was likely tucked in the magazine, just a few steps away.

When I reached the entrance of the train, a staff member blocked my way.

"No boarding."

"Oh, I'm not boarding—it's just that I left something on the train."

"Sorry, miss, the train has been cleared."

"No, please. I just need to get one little thing. If you'll just give me a second, I'm sure that it will only take a minute."

"I'm sorry, no one can board after the train has been cleared."

"Couldn't you make an exception just this once?" I looked into his eyes. "I will look like such a fool if you don't."

He sighed and pulled out a walkie-talkie. "Security."

It shocked me that he would summon security so fast. Now, not only was I going to look foolish in front of Max, I might even be reprimanded by security. I decided I couldn't let that happen.

"What's that over there?" I pointed down beside the train. "Is that someone's pet?"

He looked down. I was fairly certain that what I saw was someone's wig, but he didn't know that.

While he took a closer look, I hopped right onto the train. I just had to get back to my seat and then back off the train quickly. Everything would be fine.

The only problem was, I couldn't remember which seats we'd been in. They weren't marked well, and I didn't pay much attention when we'd left the train. One by one, I checked the seat pockets of each seat I passed. Finally, I felt the glossy pages of the magazine. I flipped it open to find nothing inside.

"No!" I groaned.

"Miss!" The staff member who had blocked me from the train stood at the end of the aisle. I gasped and turned the other way. A security officer stood at the other end. There was no way out.

"Oh dear, I got a little turned around. I'm sorry." I gulped as the security officer began to walk toward me.

"Please remain calm." He held up one hand in front of him.

"I'm trying." I frowned. "Please, I just made a little mistake."

"Where are you traveling from?" The security officer frowned.

"I'm on a tour."

"What kind of tour?" He raised an eyebrow.

"A book tour."

"I knew it!" The man behind me shouted. I jumped and inched closer to the security officer.

"Single Wide Female, right?" He grinned.

"Uh—yes." I looked between the two men.

"My wife loves your books." The staff member clapped her on the shoulder. "She told me you might be on board and begged me to try to get your autograph."

"Oh well, I'd be happy to do that. Maybe off the train?"

"Sure. Come right along."

He led me off the train. The security guard followed after us. I could hear his heavy footsteps. Would he arrest me?

When I reached the bottom of the steps, Max held out his hand to me.

"Sammy." He shook his head, but before he could say more, the security guard held out some papers to me.

"These are yours."

I braced myself for what the consequences might be. The worst part was I hadn't even found the itinerary.

CHAPTER 2

My hand trembled as I took the documents from the security guard. Once I had them in my hand, I looked down to see that it was a full copy of my itinerary and car rental voucher.

"How did you get this?"

"I called security to bring some replacement documents," the staff member said. "I would have told you, but when I turned around you were gone. Now about that autograph?"

"Thank you so much for your help. Here." I signed the paper he held out to me. "Tell your wife if she wants to attend any of my sessions, she'll be welcome."

"She'll be ecstatic that I met you! The car rental is over there." He pointed me in the right direction.

I gripped the papers tightly as I walked toward the rental.

Max caught up with me, tugging the luggage cart behind him.

"What was all of that about?"

"I thought I could find the papers."

"But you could have been arrested. We're in different countries now—you can't always get away with things like that."

"Ah, but I did." I winked at him and paused at the counter.

Max rested the cart against the counter and turned toward me. "Listen, if you're going to do something like that, at least fill me in first, okay?"

"Okay." I smiled at him and kissed the tip of his nose. "Sorry I worried you."

He opened his mouth to say more, but an attendant walked up to the counter.

"Is there something I can help you with?"

"We have a rental reservation." I slid the papers to him.

"Ah, yes. Oh." He frowned. He typed something into the computer, then looked up at me. "I think there may have been a mix-up."

"I'm sorry?" I frowned. "What kind of mix-up?"

"What we have reserved for you is a motorbike."

"Not a car?" I shook my head. "I don't think that will do."

"I'm sorry. It's all we have left at the moment. I could call you a taxi instead…"

"No, it's fine." Max smiled and reached out for the keys. "We'll take it."

"What are you talking about, Max?" I looked over at him.

"I'm sure it's temporary. Isabella will get it all straightened out."

"But I can't drive a motorbike—and what will we do with our luggage?"

"I can drive it, and I'm sure we can have our luggage delivered to the hotel. Right?" He looked back at the attendant.

"Absolutely—right away."

I hesitated. I didn't like when things didn't go as planned.

Max grinned. "What's wrong? Don't trust me?"

"Of course I trust you."

"Then let's ride, baby." He swept his arm around my waist and tugged me toward the parking lot.

I tried to think of a few different excuses to make him change his mind. It wasn't that I didn't trust Max, I just wasn't sure that riding around a new country on a motorbike was the best idea.

Another attendant met Max in the parking lot with two helmets.

"Make sure they're fastened well."

"Not a problem." Max smiled and pushed the helmet down on top of my head. He tugged the chinstrap tight. "How's that?"

"Snug."

"Perfect." He donned his own helmet. "Ready?"

"As I'll ever be." I looked from him to the motorbike. It looked more like a dirt bike to me—much smaller than a regular motorcycle. "This is for both of us? How are we going to fit?"

"Well, that's the best part." Max met my eyes. "You're going to have to get in close to me and hold on tight." He hopped on and patted the seat behind him.

I laughed and climbed on to the back of the bike. Maybe it wasn't what I would have normally done in the situation—I probably would have accepted the taxi—but the joy in Max's eyes couldn't be replaced by the comfort of a taxi. I wrapped my arms around his waist and realized just why he thought it would be a good idea. It was wonderful to hold him so close as he roared out of the parking lot.

Venice flew by me as Max sped down the road. I tried to catch a glimpse or two of the things that I passed, but there was too much to see without stopping.

When we finally did stop, it was in front of a majestic hotel. I was a little surprised by the size of it. Its steepled roof seemed to scream romance.

Max helped me off the back of the motorbike.

"See? That wasn't so bad, was it?" He smiled at me.

"Ask me when my legs stop wobbling." I grinned and looped my arm through his. "I wouldn't have wanted to do it with anyone else."

"Good to know." He guided me to the door of the hotel.

When Max opened the door the bright light of the

lobby greeted me. A lovely scent filled the air. The warmth of the lobby, combined with the lilt of peaceful music that filtered through speakers in each corner of the room, enveloped me with a sense of warmth.

"It's beautiful." I leaned my head against Max's shoulder and squeezed his arm.

"Made even more beautiful by your presence." He winked at me as we walked up to the front desk.

I gave the woman behind the desk the information for the reservation.

"Ah yes, the honeymoon suite."

"Are you sure? It should just be a regular room." I frowned as I tried to peer around her at the computer screen.

"No mistake. Isabella insisted. She said that you and your husband should be treated to anything that you'd like, so feel free to peruse the room service menu." She handed me a set of key cards. "These will let you into the room as well as the pool, the spa, and the gym."

"Wow! We don't need to leave the hotel." Max laughed.

"Only for the book signing. There will be some information on the sessions in your room. Isabella will try to meet you both for dinner. Her schedule is a bit busier than she'd expected. Until then, if you need anything just ring the front desk."

"Thank you." I handed one of the keys to Max.

"Have fun." The woman smiled. "I'm looking

forward to your book signing."

I nodded to her and smiled again. It was amazing to me how many fans I'd already run into. Maybe it would be a small amount to an actual celebrity, but to me it was huge.

CHAPTER 3

We rode the elevator up to the top floor.

Max glanced over at me. "Are you excited?"

"Very—and a little nervous."

"You'll get used to it. By the time the tour is over, you'll be a pro."

"I hope so." I smiled and took Max's hand as we stepped off the elevator.

Instead of stepping off into a hallway, we stepped into a foyer that led directly into the honeymoon suite. The living space was filled with overstuffed furniture and marble décor.

"Wow, look at this place. Maybe we should call Isabella and make sure that this isn't a mistake. Can you imagine how much this cost?"

"Sh, don't worry about that." Max wrapped his arms around me. "This is your life now, Sammy, and it's only going to get better. You're in demand, and the more popular you become, the more luxury you're going to be surrounded by."

"But what if I don't want that?" I turned around slowly as I took in the full impact of my beautiful surroundings. "What if all this makes me uncomfortable?"

Max slid his hands into his pockets and studied me. After a few moments he frowned.

"What is it?" he asked. "Do you think you don't deserve this?"

I shrugged. "I don't know. Maybe."

"You deserve all this and more." He brushed his hand across my shoulder and turned me to face him. "You've done all of this on your own. You've generated this desire in people to provide you with an amazing experience. How could that make you uncomfortable?"

I sighed and looked into his eyes. "I don't know, but it does. Maybe I have this feeling—like if I get used to it, it's all going to disappear."

He leaned forward and kissed my forehead. "No one knows what the future will bring, but the important things—what we feel for one another and the impact you seem to be having on women around the world—those things will never disappear. So relax and enjoy it. Hm? If you worry yourself over it, then in five years when you look back you're going to wonder why you didn't just enjoy this moment."

"How did you get so wise?" I brushed my fingertips along the curve of his cheek.

"I learned it from you, I think."

"Ha. I doubt it."

"And that's the problem." He kissed my forehead again. "You have to find a way to wash that doubt right out of your system, Sammy."

"You're right." I frowned and looked down at my feet. "Sometimes I really wonder how I can give advice to other women when I still struggle so much myself."

"That's when someone gives the best advice, don't you think? These women aren't looking for someone to tell them what to do. They're looking for someone who feels what they feel. Can I tell you something?"

"Of course." I looked back up into his eyes.

"You promise not to argue with me?"

"Uh." I grinned.

"You promise that you'll try not to argue with me?" He winked.

"Yes, I'll try."

"Sammy, I've never—not for a second—doubted you." He smiled and pulled me close to him. "I know that you have a hard time believing that, but it's the truth. You turned my world upside down the day I met you. You still do—every time I look at you."

"How did I get so lucky?" I sighed and hugged him.

"That's what I ask myself." He kissed the side of my neck. "We're lucky we have each other—and this moment—and this amazing experience. I'm sure that we can think of a few ways to enjoy it."

"Oh yes, I believe we can." I laughed as he tugged me toward the bedroom.

A few hours later I smoothed down the black skirt of my cocktail dress. In the mirror it looked too tight. My legs were too exposed. My shoulders peeked out of the capped sleeves. Should I change? I tugged at one of the sleeves.

"You look gorgeous." Max stepped out of the bathroom in a gray jacket that made his eyes shine. "Ready to go?"

"I'm not sure." I stared into the mirror for a few more seconds. "I think maybe I should change."

He glanced at his watch. "We don't really have time. You look perfect just like that. What's the problem?"

I took a deep breath and remembered our conversation from earlier in the day. I had to stop doubting myself so much. Instead of seeing the flaws of the dress, I forced myself to see the parts I liked. The skirt flattered my hips. The neckline was dramatic without being classless. The fine detail along the hem was what drew me to the dress in the first place.

"Okay, let's go." I grabbed my purse and hurried away from the mirror before I could change my mind.

In the elevator on the way down to the lobby, I noticed Max as he tugged at the sleeve of his jacket. First one, then the other. Then he straightened his tie. I smiled to myself as I realized that maybe he had his own doubts.

"You look great, Max."

He glanced over at me with surprise. "Thanks."

"I mean it." I trailed a hand down along the sleeve of his jacket, then took his hand in mine. "I can't wait to show you off."

"Oh, really?" He grinned and took a step closer to me.

"Yes, really." I leaned in for a kiss just as the elevator doors slid open.

CHAPTER 4

"I see you're enjoying Italy."

Isabella was standing there grinning at us as the elevator doors slid open.

I pulled away from Max and as I did I stumbled on my high heel. Max reached out to catch me but only managed to grab my arm on the way down. I still landed on my rear end right in front of Isabella and about twenty other people who were waiting to board the elevator.

"Sammy, are you okay?" Max pulled me back to my feet.

I couldn't look at Isabella. My cheeks burned so hot that I knew any make-up I put on was wasted. "I'm okay." I hurried off the elevator so that the people who were waiting could get on.

Max kept one hand on my lower back. Whether it was to prevent another fall or offer me support didn't really matter. I appreciated it.

"That was quite a tumble. You didn't twist your ankle, did you?" Isabella looked down at my ankle with concern—my huge ankles.

"I'm fine. I'm sorry. I feel so foolish."

"Don't feel that way. I shouldn't have startled you. We have a table reserved in the restaurant here."

"I want to thank you for the incredible room. It's really much more than we expected."

"Good. I wanted it to be. You should be able to enjoy yourself while you're here. I want this to be a memory for you, not just a leg of your tour."

"It certainly is." I smiled.

As we sat down at the table, I tried to let go of the embarrassment of my fall in the elevator. I needed to focus on the moment.

Isabella ordered a fine wine, then looked across the table at me. "So there have been some changes to our itinerary."

"Oh?" I took a sip of the wine that the waiter delivered.

"Yes, unfortunately the book signing I had lined up at a local bookstore got shot down."

"Oh, no." My eyes widened.

"It turns out that they had a bit of a bug problem and have been forced to fumigate. It's horrifying, I know." She sighed. "But I managed to book us a venue. It's not quite what you're used to, though."

"What is it?" I braced myself. Would it be in a school cafeteria somewhere? Would it be on a street corner?

"As you know, your book is very popular, and even more so here in Venice. I put my feelers out to local events that would be able to handle the turnout I'm expecting, and one event in particular practically begged me for the opportunity to host you."

"Oh, how nice." My heart fluttered.

Max took my hand under the table and gave it a squeeze.

"There's a small fashion show taking place tomorrow. It is an intimate gathering, but it's very selective—invite only. Alistair—the man in charge—offered to open up the venue prior to the fashion show, for all our guests."

"A fashion show?" I frowned. Even the street corner sounded better than that. "Do you really think that's an appropriate setting?"

"What could be better?" Isabella raised an eyebrow. "You inspire people to see their beauty, and a fashion show is all about beauty."

"It's not that I'm not grateful for the opportunity—I really am—but it just seems to me that a fashion show only perpetuates one kind of beauty…and I doubt that many of my readers could identify with that type of beauty." I frowned. "I'm sorry, I'm not sure it's a good idea."

"Perhaps you need to get to know all of your readers, Samantha." Isabella paused as the waiter returned to take our orders.

The tone of her voice lingered with me. Had I offended her? My stomach churned. I really wasn't getting off to a great start with Isabella, between the fall and then my response to her idea. After all she'd done to make us feel comfortable, I shouldn't be difficult.

"You know what, Isabella, you're right. I'm sorry. I guess I was just a little surprised. I'm sure you know best what would be a good venue. So if you think this is the right way to go, then I'm all for it."

Isabella smiled at me. "I think you're going to love it. In fact, Alistair has even invited you to be part of the runway show."

"What?" My eyes widened.

"You really must. It would be fantastic publicity."

I could barely hear her voice. A loud roar rushed through my head. Walk a runway in Venice? In front of all of those people? How could I ever do something like that? I looked over at Max.

He smiled as he looked back at me. "You'll be wonderful."

I wanted to punch him right in the nose. Okay, maybe not punch him, but I wanted to knock some sense into him. Max, always supportive, said what he thought he was supposed to say, but I didn't want to hear that. I wanted him to share in my absolute horror at the thought.

"Just let me know, so we can get a dress fitted for you." Isabella smiled at the waiter as he brought our food.

When he set my plate down in front of me, all I saw was butter and calories. What was I thinking when I ordered it? Well, I certainly wasn't thinking about walking down a runway. My mind blurred as I thought about how

I'd gone off my diet in France. I'd likely gained back a few pounds—maybe more than a few.

"I think it's a great idea." Max picked up his fork and dug into his meal.

I kicked his foot under the table. He jumped and looked over at me with a raised eyebrow. "It's great publicity, like Isabella said."

"Sure." I forced a smile. "Let me just think about it, okay?"

"I'll need an answer by the morning so that we can get the dress ready." Isabella leaned across the table slightly and looked into my eyes. "Trust me, you want to wear this dress. It's the newest in his line and it is gorgeous. I just know it will be stunning on you."

CHAPTER 5

I bit into my bottom lip and looked down at the food on my plate again. I didn't share Isabella's confidence, but wasn't that the problem? As Max pointed out, I needed to believe in myself, not constantly give in to doubt.

"Alright. Yes, I'll do it. Of course I will." I laughed a little. "How could I turn down such an incredible opportunity?"

"Wonderful!" Isabella pulled out her phone. "I'll just send the designer a text now. In the morning you'll need to meet with his staff to get fitted for the dress, okay? I'll send a car for you. I heard that there was a mix-up about the vehicles. I'm so sorry about that."

"It was fine." I tried to control my pounding heart. "Max and I enjoyed the ride. Didn't we, Max?"

"We sure did." He pointed to my plate. "Is your food okay? You haven't taken a bite. Should I call the waiter over?"

"No, it's fine. It's delicious." I picked up my fork and let it hover over the food. My mind filled with images of me waddling down the runway as butter sauce dripped down my chin. I knew it was a little ridiculous to think that way, but that was the image that made me put my fork back down. "I think I'm just a little worn out from traveling. Maybe I'll take mine to go."

Max locked eyes with me, but he didn't argue. He signaled for the waiter and asked for my food to be boxed. I was relieved that he didn't push me on the issue.

Isabella and I got caught up in a lively conversation about the assortment of activities Max and I could enjoy while in Venice. By the time the check was paid, I'd forgotten about my nerves—until my stomach growled with hunger. I grasped the take-home container, and the scent of the food within it made my stomach growl again.

Max took the container from me.

"Thanks for dinner, Isabella." I smiled at her.

"I wish you could have enjoyed it. Do tell me if you're getting ill. I'm sure we can arrange some time for you to rest."

"I'll be fine." I took Max's free hand in mine. "I think I just need to let my stomach settle a little from the train."

"Have a good evening. I'll text you first thing in the morning, and I'll make sure the car I send is actually a car."

"Great. Thank you so much."

Max led me toward the elevator. As soon as we were by ourselves, he looked over at me. "What's going on with you?"

"What do you mean?"

"Please, Sammy, I can tell when you're hungry. Your face gets pale, your voice is softer—I know you." He narrowed his eyes. "You ordered one of your favorites, so why didn't you eat?"

I quirked an eyebrow. Having Max along on the book tour was great, but he didn't let me get away with anything.

"I just wasn't hungry."

He pursed his lips. From the tremble in his jaw I was sure he wanted to question me further, but the elevator doors slid open. He stepped aside as a family stepped off, then held the doors open for me. Luckily, a few other people stepped onto the elevator as well, which prevented the conversation from continuing. Then, floor by floor, people stepped off the elevator, until we were alone.

He looked over at me. "I'm worried. Should I be worried?"

I pointed to the elevator doors as they slid open. "Let's go in."

He followed after me and set down the food in the kitchen. I was ready to dig in, but the thought of the dress the next morning made me shudder.

Max ran his hands down from my shoulders to my elbows and up again. "Talk to me. What's going on?"

"I'm sorry, Max. I feel like everything I built up—every little bit of confidence—is gone." I sighed and turned to face him. "I'm not sure if I can go through with this runway walk."

"Is that why you didn't eat?" He narrowed his eyes. "Sammy, you know better than that. Starving yourself is never acceptable."

"I know, I know." I plopped down in one of the chairs at the table and flipped open the container. "Grab me a fork, will you?"

"Gladly." He sat down beside me and handed me the fork. "Now tell me what's got you so rattled."

"I was looking at this magazine on the train—at all of these beautiful Italian women. I mean, I know that beauty is different for everyone, but this beauty is a beauty I could never attain."

"No one's asking you to change how you look, Sammy. That's what you're getting stuck on. The people here know your beauty—they see it and they want the world to see it too." He stole a bit of my food. "I think you need a refresher. Maybe you should do some blogging."

"Maybe." I frowned. My stomach stopped churning as I filled it with the delicious food.

CHAPTER 6

It embarrassed me to think that I was willing to go without food because of a dress. My readers deserved more than that from me. I deserved more.

I turned to look at Max, who was watching me while I ate. "I just wish I could feel like I belonged, I guess. I don't think I'll ever feel that way."

"What do you mean, you want to belong?"

"You know what I mean. Fit in—like I could just blend into the background and be a part of the crowd."

Max laughed so loud that I glared at him.

"What's so funny about that?"

"Sammy, you could never blend in."

"Oh." I furrowed a brow. I wasn't sure exactly what he was getting at, but his words weren't hitting me the right way. "Okay…"

"Why would you want to? You're a vivacious, creative, bold person. You are never going to fit into anyone's mold, which is one of the millions of reasons that I love you. Why would you ever want to be like anyone else?" Max shook his head. "Maybe I have the wrong idea about what you want, but I never even considered the idea that you'd want to fit in."

"Of course I do. It's hard to stick out like a sore thumb. I'm so clumsy, and I'm always getting into strange predicaments." I frowned. "Doesn't that bother you?"

"No, Sammy." He took my hand and looked into my eyes. "No, it doesn't—not for a second. The only thing that ever bothers me is you thinking that you're anything less than perfect. I don't know how to explain that to you."

"I'm trying."

"I know you are." He kissed the back of my hand. "And so are all of the women out there that are waiting to hear from you. Are you going to tell them that they should find a way to fit in—like all of the magazines do, like the media does—or are you going to inspire them to be proud and stand out?"

I frowned. "I hate it when you're right."

"You don't."

"I do."

"You love it." He grinned and gave my hand a squeeze. "It happens so rarely."

"Oh, stop."

"So? You didn't answer."

"I would never tell a woman to try to blend in. You're right. I guess I'm having a hard time accepting this new role I'm in. I feel like I have to look the part of a successful woman to deserve the success that I'm experiencing."

"You deserve it because of who you are. You got yourself here—no one else did that for you."

"You might have helped a little." I grinned at him.

"Maybe, but sometimes I've pushed against it too. You've stuck to your guns. You've known what you wanted and you've been going for it. That's pretty amazing. Don't lose that now out of fear. You have to stick it out and keep going."

"Maybe some sleep will help me with that."

"Good idea. Why don't you take a nice warm bath first? That tub looks great."

"Excellent." I cleaned up after my dinner, then walked to the bedroom and the bathroom connected to it.

As the water ran into the large round tub, I tried to focus on calming my nerves. I didn't need to be anything more than what I was. That was one of the hardest lessons I'd ever faced—that somehow I was already perfect.

When I climbed into the tub, I was sure that I'd be feeling exhausted, but the warmth of the water actually cleared my mind. Old habits were hard to avoid. I could remember times when I thought eating as little as possible was the way to lose the weight I battled. I treated my body horribly, and my body responded by getting sick and sluggish. It was easy to think that a missed meal or two would lead to progress in my weight loss, but it actually had the opposite affect. What was I so scared of that I was falling back into such harmful habits?

I closed my eyes. There it was—the runway—well lit and surrounded by an audience. There I was, in a dress so tight I was nothing but rolls. I toddled down the runway on high heels far too high for me.

Suddenly, I understood my fear. It wasn't so much that I wanted to fit in, it was more that I would be forced to. Someone else would choose my dress and my shoes. Someone else would tell me what was acceptable and not acceptable.

As this realization hit me, I knew what my real challenge was. I needed to be strong enough to stand up for my own beauty as I saw it, rather than allowing someone else to shape it to suit them.

The next morning I woke up with butterflies in my stomach. I could smell lemon and mint. Max had made tea. I smiled as I climbed out of bed. I couldn't imagine being on the tour without him.

When I walked into the kitchen Max turned around with a big blueberry muffin.

"Isabella had them sent up."

"I don't know—"

"You're going to need your strength. Who knows when you're going to get another chance to eat?"

"Alright, but no butter."

"These don't need it, trust me." He handed me the

muffin along with a cup of tea.

I glanced at the clock on the microwave. "Did she say what time we have to be there?"

"In a half hour."

"What? That's not enough time!"

"All you have to do is show up and they will dress you, so no need to rush." Max tapped the side of the cup. "I thought tea might be better than coffee."

"Good idea." I smiled and sipped the tea. The warm liquid did wonders to soothe the anxiety within me, but my mind kept shifting to the fitting. Would I have any say in how it fit? What if it looked ridiculous on me? Would I be able to say no? The last thing I wanted to do was offend Isabella.

I made the decision that I'd be cooperative and have the best attitude I could muster about the whole experience.

CHAPTER 7

When I finished my food, I threw on some comfortable clothes and met Max at the elevator.

"Do you mind if I go exploring a bit while you're at the fitting?" He pushed the button for the lobby.

"No, of course not. Are you going to take the motorbike?"

"Yes. I'll be careful."

"Good." I kissed him goodbye in the lobby, then headed for the car that waited at the curb.

Once inside I took a deep breath. If I could hold things together long enough to get through the fitting then I knew everything would be fine.

The car stopped in front of a towering building. I stared up at the multitude of windows and wondered which office held the designer. I didn't have to wonder long as a young woman walked up to me.

"Samantha?" She popped bright pink gum that matched the color of her hair.

"Yes."

"I'm Sue." She held out one hand and as I shook it, I

noticed she kept the other hand in the folds of her coat. "Come with me. Daniella is waiting for you."

"Daniella?"

"She's the one who will fit the dress to you."

"I hope they're prepared to add plenty of material."

"Oh, nonsense, I'm sure you'll look beautiful in it." She raised an eyebrow. "A beautiful dress is made beautiful by the confidence of the woman who wears it."

"Do you think so?"

"No, but you do." She laughed. "I read that in your book."

"Oh, right, of course." I smiled at her. She had a very petite frame and likely wasn't much taller than five feet. Her pink curls were adorable and her bright green eyes made me wonder if that shade even existed in nature. How gorgeous. I smiled to myself as she led me into the building.

When we stepped into the elevator I noticed that she used her right hand to push the button, while her left hand remained tucked away. On the third floor we stepped off and into a long hallway.

"It's the third office on the right." She gestured and as she did, her coat unfolded. For just a moment I caught a glimpse of her left hand. There were two fingers and a portion of a thumb. She tucked her hand away again as soon as she noticed the direction of my gaze.

"I'm sorry." I gulped. "I wasn't staring."

"It's okay." She smiled. "I'm used to it. It's a birth

defect, not a Mafia debt—I swear."

I laughed but I wondered if I should have.

With her hand still hidden she moved toward the office door.

"Wait, Sue."

"Yes?" She turned back to me.

"I was curious about why you were hiding your hand. I just want you to know, you shouldn't have to hide it from me. Your hand is unique. It's beautiful."

"Thanks for saying that, but to be honest, it makes most people uncomfortable. So I just try to keep it hidden. It makes things easier on other people."

"Doesn't it bother you to hide a part of yourself?"

"No, not really. When I was younger I was bullied a bit for it, so I just learned how to keep it to myself."

"I'm sorry that you experienced that."

"It was what it was." She smiled. "People are much more polite as adults. Go ahead in. Daniella is waiting."

I nodded and stepped inside.

"Samantha? So glad you're here. We need to get started right away. Please take your clothes off."

I stared at the woman before me. She was the polar opposite of Sue. Her stature towered over even mine. Her hips and shoulders spread just as wide. She carried a good amount of weight. The pants suit she wore flattered her shape, and the wide smile on her lips gave me the impression that she was a friendly person.

"Uh, maybe in another room?"

"Please, there's no need to be shy around me. We really don't have time for niceties."

"Okay." I frowned as I began to tug off my shirt. I still found it difficult to be naked most of the time. I'd gotten fairly used to it around Max, but in front of a complete stranger was a different story.

Daniella busied herself with a dress. Once I was ready, she held the dress up to me.

"Oh no, that's going to be too small."

"Trust me, just try it on." She held it out to me.

"No, I don't want to tear it."

"Samantha, I've been in this business for over fifteen years. I can look at you and know not just your size, but your exact measurements. Trust me and try it on." She shook the dress.

"It's not my fault if it rips."

"It won't."

I sighed and eased the dress over my head. It was a little tough to get it down past my shoulders, but Daniella helped. Once it was over my chest it was much easier.

"Ah, perfect." Daniella clapped her hands together. "I knew it would be."

I turned toward the large mirror on the wall. From the tension in the dress I expected to look like a sausage. Instead, by some miracle, the dress seemed to be clinging in all the right places.

CHAPTER 8

"Wow." I stared at my reflection.

"I know. It's amazing what the designer has done. So many designers only design for one body type. But you and I both know that women come in many different shapes and sizes. I've done so many fittings on models, and I'll admit to some jealousy that I would never be able to wear what they were wearing. One day the designer looked at me and asked me if I wanted to try on one of the dresses. When I laughed in his face, he was offended. He ranted at me, and I really thought I'd lost my job." She smoothed the skirt over my hip. "But the next morning he was in my office with a few garments for me to try. He told me that he could make any woman look stunning, and he meant it. So he experimented with me a bit and tried to get me on the runway. I'm just not the type to do that." She shook her head and laughed. "The last thing I want is a bunch of cameras flashing in my face. So you get that honor, my dear."

"Thanks—I think." I smiled into the mirror.

"You wear it beautifully. I'm just going to do a few little touch-ups and it will be ready for you by noon. Oh, and tonight's going to be spectacular—truly a wonderful event."

"Tonight? I thought the fashion show was at noon?"

"Oh, that little thing? Yes it is, but the designer invited you to walk down the runway at the main show tonight."

"What do you mean by main show?"

Daniella lifted her eyebrows. "I mean that it will be televised, and the elite of the elite will be there."

"I don't understand. Then what is happening at noon?"

"At noon it's just a pre-show. It's a demonstration of what he has to offer—mostly to high-end clients."

"This is unbelievable." I shook my head. "I can't do this. There's no way."

"You have to do it. Look at yourself." Daniella placed one hand on her hip. "It fits you just right."

"There is a very high likelihood that I will fall flat on my face."

"Oh, don't say that."

"No, I'm serious. I speak from experience. I have a very hard time staying upright, especially in high heels." I sighed and looked back at my reflection in the mirror.

"Samantha, no one else would do that dress justice. It looks like it was made for you. This is an opportunity to represent real women on the runway. Can you really let that opportunity pass you by?"

I frowned. In my heart her words made sense, but my brain was full of questions. "Why wouldn't you do it?"

"I don't want to be known." She shrugged. "I want the world to know me for my clothing, not for my face. I'm more of a behind-the-scenes type. I have my own designs that I want to make public, and when they're ready, they'll make it to the runway."

"I can understand that." I smiled. "I can't wait to see some of your work."

"It will be soon, trust me. But there's a much better chance of me being able to break into the mainstream fashion world if someone like you in that amazing dress walks down the runway. You'll be doing more than just promoting your book, Samantha. You're going to be creating a niche in the fashion industry, an opportunity for every woman to be represented on the runway. I really thought you'd be excited about it."

"I know." I clasped my hands together. "I should be. I'm trying to be. But the thought of parading around in front of people...I don't know. I spent so much of my life trying to hide all my trouble spots and now I'm supposed to put them on display?"

"Sweetheart, you don't have any trouble spots. You look gorgeous." Daniella looked into my eyes. "Your book talks about confidence. If you push yourself to get through this experience, imagine the confidence boost you'll have."

"Hm. I hope so." I took a deep breath and closed my eyes. "Of course I'm going to do this. I can't turn down such a great opportunity. I just don't know if I'll make it down the runway in one piece."

"Go enjoy your day for a few hours. That's the best thing to do. I get nervous before every show that I've done alterations in. Trust me, a wardrobe malfunction can mean the end of my career."

My eyes widened at the thought of a wardrobe malfunction. It was something that I hadn't even considered.

"Does that happen often?"

"Not with me, but with others, I've seen it. It's never pretty when a garment falls apart on the runway." She gasped. "Oh no, I shouldn't be talking to you about this, should I? Samantha, that's not going to happen to you. I promise. I'll be very careful with the dress."

"I guess I'd better get it off, then, so you can get to it." I started to pull the dress off. As snug as it was on my chest and shoulders going on, coming off was even worse.

"Here, let me help." Daniella's hands freed me from the stranglehold the dress had me in.

I took a deep breath as soon as I could.

"Thanks!"

"Don't worry. It'll be an easier fit later. Go have fun. Forget everything that I've said. It's all going to be perfect."

I gathered up my clothes and hurried to dress. I planned to take Daniella's advice. Maybe a little fun would distract me from all the anxiety that seemed to be steadily building within me.

As soon as I was out of the building, I called Max's cell phone.

"Done already?"

"Yes. Any chance you're anywhere nearby?"

"You tell me where you are, and I'll be there in minutes."

"I'll send you the address."

I texted him the address, then took a look around. There were a few small shops nearby, but that wasn't what caught my interest. It was the people that walked past me on the sidewalk. Many walked with a very distinct attitude, a sense of confidence—as if they were exactly where they were supposed to be at any given moment. That was the type of confidence I'd been chasing after. Many times I'd come close to it, but it was difficult to maintain.

The roar of the motorcycle engine distracted me from my observations. I turned to find Max at the curb.

"How did it go?" He offered me my helmet.

I took it with a smile.

"Let's just say, it's a little more than I'd expected. I'll fill you in soon. I promise. I just don't want to think about it right now. I want to use the time we have before the book signing to share some of Venice with you."

"That sounds great. Hop on."

CHAPTER 9

I tightened my helmet and climbed on the motorcycle behind Max. As he drove off, a surge of freedom rushed through me. In that moment I believed that I could accomplish anything.

He pulled down a side street and then into a parking space along the water.

"I hope you don't mind. I had an idea of what we might be able to do. It won't take too long, and I hope it will relax you a little."

"I don't mind. I trust anything you come up with."

He led me toward a small dock. Just as we walked up, a gondola slid into place.

"Wow, Max what a great idea. This will give us a chance to see so much in a short time."

"I thought it would be perfect for today." He smiled and took my hand.

The gondolier gestured for both of us to board.

Max helped me into the flat-bottomed boat, then stepped in himself. When the boat wobbled a little, I hurried to sit down on the cushioned seat. I didn't want to risk toppling over the side. Max settled beside me and laced his fingers around mine. A moment later the gondola slid across the smooth water.

I looked up at the buildings that surrounded us. There was something so whimsical about the sight of them. The easy way the boat slid between them made the entire experience seem like a dream. Only the warmth of Max's hand around mine grounded me in reality.

From one of the upper windows a melody drifted down to us. It was light, with bursts of piano followed by fast-paced violin. As I closed my eyes and listened to the music, my muscles relaxed. The tension that had been brewing within me eased. I leaned my head against Max's shoulder and looked up at the sky.

"Look where you've brought us, Sammy." He kissed the top of my head. "We wouldn't be experiencing this if it weren't for your success."

"You're just as much to blame." I winked at him and stole a quick kiss.

He laughed and wrapped his arm around my shoulders.

As I settled against his chest, I watched Venice glide past. Max was right. I never would have ended up in such a beautiful place if it weren't for the book tour. That just reinforced within me that I needed to get with the program. Even if it did make me a little uncomfortable, the opportunities that were being presented to me were rare. I was lucky to have them.

I closed my eyes again. This time I heard a different sound. It was a strange chirp. When I opened my eyes, I noticed the chirp seemed to be coming from just beside the boat. I peered down into the water, curious what the sound was. There was nothing in the water that I could see. The chirp then came from the other side of the boat.

"Do you hear that, Max? What is it?"

"I'm not sure." Max peered around. "Maybe some kind of bird?"

"Is everything okay?" The gondolier slowed the boat.

"I just heard a strange noise." I frowned. "I'm sure it's nothing."

"What did it sound like?"

"A chirp—kind of like a bird."

"Oh." He cleared his throat. "Let's just get back to the dock."

"Why?" I raised an eyebrow. "Is something wrong."

"Sometimes a slow leak can sound a bit like a chirp. It's best that we return to the dock."

"It's leaking?" I looked over at Max. "Are we going to sink?"

"No, I'm sure we won't. Let's just try to enjoy the ride, hm?" He pulled me close and kissed me.

I tried to enjoy the moment. I tried to savor the sensation of his lips against mine. It should have been a perfect romantic experience, but my heart was pounding for other reasons.

I'd read that the waters of Venice were quite deep. Would we have to swim? What if I cramped up? The thought made my heart race even faster.

"Sammy?" Max pulled away and looked into my eyes. "Are you okay? You're shaking."

"I want to get off at the next dock. I'm afraid we're going to sink."

Max sighed and looked up at the gondolier. "He doesn't look worried."

"Would he tell us if he was?" I whispered my words and hoped that the man wouldn't be offended if he heard them.

Max frowned. "Sir? Are we in any danger?"

"No, it may not be a leak at all. It's just better to be on the cautious side."

"See?" Max smiled and tried to draw me back into another kiss.

I relaxed and returned the kiss. How many other chances would I have to kiss Max on a gondola?

The boat dipped a bit more than I expected.

"Ouch." Max drew back and put his fingers on his bottom lip. "You bit me." He laughed around the accusation.

"I'm sorry. I didn't mean to. I just felt that dip and I thought—"

"Sorry, I was going a bit faster than usual." The gondolier frowned. "We're almost to the dock."

I didn't know if I could wait that long. My stomach

churned along with the pounding of my heart.

Max squeezed my hand. "It's going to be okay, Sammy. See, the dock's right over there." He pointed to the dock.

When I turned to look, I turned faster than I intended. The boat rocked.

The gondolier wavered. "Please, be still."

CHAPTER 10

My cheeks burned as I tried to be as still as possible, but when there was a loud shriek, I had to turn and look. The boat rocked again. This time, the gondolier more than wavered, he was about to fall off the side of the boat. I knew that it was my fault.

In a split-second, I jumped up and grabbed for his hand. He gasped as I pulled him back to safety. For an instant I was a hero. However, in the next moment, that sensation of victory was gone—and replaced by a sensation of falling.

"Sammy!" Max lunged for me.

I crashed into the water with an impact that I'm sure affected all of the gondolas in the water. As the water washed over me, I struggled to get to the surface. My shoes, my clothes—even my hair—all grew heavy. The panic that gripped me didn't help. I thrashed to keep my head above the water.

Max's hand thrust through my wild splashing and seized my wrist. He tugged hard to pull me back toward the side of the gondola.

"Climb in." Max's concerned eyes locked to mine.

"No, no! Please don't do that." The gondolier crouched down to look at me. "If you try to climb in, the entire boat can capsize. We are very near to the dock. Can you hold on until we get there?"

I nodded and hoped that the water splashing on my face hid my tears. I was sure that everyone within eyesight was staring at me. I kicked my feet a little in an attempt to help the boat along. In my mind my tumble from the boat was a clear sign that any walk down the runway for me would be a disaster.

When we reached the dock, Max climbed out of the gondola and helped me up on to the dock.

"Are you okay?" The gondolier looked me over.

"Yes, I'm okay. I'm sorry I caused so much trouble."

"You saved me." He smiled. "That was a very nice thing to do."

"Maybe, but I rocked the boat in the first place."

"If I hadn't been going so fast, we never would have had any problems. I should have checked the boat before we set out. I'm very sorry that your ride was disrupted. Please, if you would be willing, return any time for a free ride. I will make sure the gondola is in perfect shape before we set out."

I forced a smile but I couldn't imagine getting back on a gondola. I shivered as my soaked clothes clung to my body.

"Let's get you dry." Max steered me away from the

dock.

"Max, there's no way that I can do these runway shows. Look what's happened now. I can't even go for a simple boat ride without causing a disaster."

"Sammy, you're reading too much into it. You got scared, then you were brave enough to try to catch the gondolier and ended up in the water yourself. That's nothing to be ashamed of."

"It isn't?" I looked at all of the people who stared back at me as I walked toward the parking lot. "It sure seems to me that it might be."

"Sammy, what is this all about?" Max caught my hand in his. "Ever since we got here you've been doubting and second-guessing yourself. Did something happen to make you insecure? Was it something I did?"

"No, of course not. I just think maybe this tour was a bad idea." I sighed and wrung out the bottom of my shirt. "Look, Max, there are people who are meant to be in the limelight and people who aren't. I just don't think I'm one of those people who should be out in front."

He lifted his eyebrows. "Too bad."

"What?" I stared at him. Max usually came to my defense. He usually talked me out of my self-doubt. This was different.

"Too bad. You're already here. You're already in the limelight. You can't back out now."

"Sure I can. It's called booking a plane ticket."

"No, it's called a violation of a contract." He crossed

his arms. "You have no choice but to continue with the tour, or you're going to lose everything that you've worked so hard for. Is that what you want?"

"No, of course it's not what I want." I narrowed my eyes. "Why are you being so cruel?"

"I'm not being cruel. I want you to snap out of this. So you fell in the water. Yes, it happens. Yes it does seem to happen a little more often to you, but that's just part of life. We still have a job to do while we're here. My job is to keep you on track. Your job is to keep inspiring your readers. If you're not doing your job, then clearly I'm not doing my job. Something has gone wrong here, and we need to fix it." He glanced at his watch. "Fast. There isn't time for being gentle."

I frowned. I could agree with most of what he'd said, but that didn't mean that I liked it. In fact, I definitely didn't like it.

"Bullying me isn't going to fix anything."

"This isn't bullying. I know you. I know that you're far more resilient than this. This is me trying to awaken that fierceness in you. The Sammy I love won't let anything get between herself and her success." He brushed my damp hair back from my face. "You've let all of this get to you. You're still exactly who you were when you first started writing, Sammy. You're still that amazing, determined woman who completely transformed her life. That is the person who will be walking down the runway."

"No." I shook my head. "No, I'm not going to do it. Take me back to the hotel." I pulled back from his touch.

He sighed and handed me my helmet. I put it on. When I climbed onto the back of the bike, I tried not to get too close to him. I told myself it was because I didn't want to get his clothes wet, but I suspected it might be more than that. Max, my ultimate cheerleader and supporter, seemed to have no clue what I was facing.

CHAPTER 11

After a very fast shower and a rush to dress, it was time to leave for the book signing. I gathered the few items that I thought I might need. Max sat on the couch and watched my every move.

"Ready?" I looked over at him.

"There's a car waiting downstairs."

"Great." I smiled and adjusted my purse on my shoulder. "Let's get going."

"I'm not going." He sat back on the couch.

"Huh? Why not?" My stomach twisted. Without Max there I would really be a mess.

"Because I think I'm part of the reason that you're doubting yourself."

"Why would you ever think that?" I ignored the subtle tick of my watch. I needed to know what was bringing Max to that conclusion.

"I think you rely too much on me. I'm here to support you, to bolster you, but you shouldn't need it. You should be able to provide that support to yourself. I always want to give it, but I don't want you to rely on me for it. Do you understand what I mean?" He didn't move to stand up.

I stood near the door and stared at him. "No, not at all. I don't understand why you would do this to me right now when you know I'm already having a hard time." The anger that billowed in me carved my words into short snaps. "How am I supposed to make it through without you there?"

"That's my point exactly." Max stood up and ran his hands down the sides of his jeans. "You act as if you need me in order to succeed. But you don't. You've done all this yourself, and somehow you've lost sight of that. You shouldn't need to make it through. You should be able to embrace it—"

"That's a lot of shoulds, you know. I really thought you accepted me for me." I stared down at my shoes. "I guess this trip is revealing more about our relationship than I expected."

"No. Don't do that." He walked over to me and caught my arms by the elbows. "Sammy, you may not understand it right now, but I'm doing this for you. That confidence, that shine in your eyes, has always been about putting one foot in front of the other. I don't want you to lose that."

"Max, you're not making any sense. Without you there this afternoon, I'll be even more nervous—I'll be even more likely to fall flat on my face." I searched his eyes. "Please don't let me face this alone."

"You never face anything alone. I will always be with you, even if I'm not there physically. But I really believe that this is something you need to do. I know you're usually the one that figures things out, but just this once I'm asking you to trust me." He rubbed my arms from my elbows down to my wrists. "Can you do that?"

A ripple of frustration nearly drove hurtful words from my lips. I wanted to tell him that this was the absolute wrong time to be pulling such a stunt. I wanted him to understand that his theory put me in an awful position. I couldn't even imagine not having him at my side.

"Max." I frowned and pulled away from his touch. "I want you there, but it's your choice."

"Sammy, I think I'm doing the right thing." He set his jaw, but I saw it tremble.

It bothered him to see me upset. If I turned on the waterworks he'd join me, no question. But I couldn't do that to Max. If he didn't want to be there, he didn't want to be there. Without another word, I turned and stepped into the elevator. The entire ride down I expected him to text me—to ask me to wait for him. But he didn't.

When I reached the car I stalled for a few minutes. Still he didn't call or text, nor did he come rushing out the door of the hotel with an apology on his lips. By the time I was settled in the car, I no longer wanted him to come. I didn't have time to think about his sudden change. I had to focus on the task at hand.

All the women who would be attending my book signing would not be there to see a heartbroken woman. I had to play the part.

When I stepped into the building, Isabella walked up to greet me with a wide smile. The smile faded the closer she got to me.

"Samantha, are you alright?" She met my eyes, her brow creased with concern.

"I'm just a little tired today."

"Are you sure you're not sick? You weren't eating last night and now you're not looking so well." She shook her head. "You shouldn't feel that you have to sacrifice your health for this."

"I'm okay." I took a deep breath. "I promise." I managed a brighter smile.

"Great, because we have a lot of people attending today. I thought you might want to meet the designer as well. He won't be here until after the book signing."

"Isabella, when I went to my fitting today, Daniella told me that I'm expected to walk in a show tonight as well? Is that true? I assumed she must be confused."

Daniella paused near the table set up for me. She looked over at me with a guilty smile. "I'm sorry, I just didn't want you to be nervous. I thought once you saw how fabulous you did at the pre-show you'd be more willing to walk tonight. The designer hoped you would, but I didn't make any promises. It has to be up to you." She tilted her head to the side and looked behind me.

"Where's Max?"

"Oh, he decided to stay at the hotel."

"I see." She nodded. "I know what that kind of tired feels like. Are you two on the outs?"

"No. Well—maybe." I shook my head. "I don't know."

"Try not to fret. You and Max are really putting yourselves through it with all this travel. You're bound to have some tiffs." She patted my cheek. "But I can see how strong the two of you are. You'll be fine."

"I hope so." I nodded. "Maybe we should just get started."

"Great. Now, I want you to do a reading, but keep it short. This group of ladies would probably appreciate a lengthier question and answer period, if you'd be willing to do that." She gestured to the chair behind my table. "Hopefully this will be comfortable for you. Also, I'm having some chilled bottled water brought in. Anything else you might need?"

Max. I closed my eyes for a moment and wondered if I'd said his name out loud. "No. Thank you, Isabella. This will be perfect."

"Great." She gave my shoulder a squeeze. "Don't worry, I'm sure that everything will work out."

CHAPTER 12

I swallowed hard. It embarrassed me that things in my life were so out of balance. Not only had I gained some weight back, but my confidence was almost zero, and now my relationship with Max was on the rocks. Sure, we'd figure it out. The question was, why was this happening now?

Max had pointed out that since we'd arrived in Venice, my confidence had taken a nosedive. I didn't have time to think about why.

As I sorted through the books on the table, I tried to practice a few affirmations. Positive thoughts generated a sense of well-being that I really needed in that moment. As I worked my way through the affirmations, I heard them in Max's voice, which didn't really seem to be helping me at all.

Every time I heard his voice in my head, a spike of anger rushed through me. *Why aren't you here with me, Max?* I took another deep breath and tried to recite some mantras in my head. As I relaxed in the repetition of the mantra, the sound of footsteps roused me.

I opened my eyes to see a man before me. He was very slender, with a tailored suit that gave him more of a figure than I'd seen on many women. From behind purple-tinted glasses he stared at me.

"Samantha?"

"Yes." I smiled. "Did you want a book signed?"

"No, I just want to look at you. Could you stand up, please?"

The request was a little strange, but I didn't want to argue. I stood up and rested my hands on the table.

"Step away from the table, please." He perched two fingertips on the slope of his chin, which was peppered with silver stubble.

"Is something wrong?" My body tensed. Most of my fans were women. Why was this man so interested in what I looked like?

"Not if you do as I ask. Step out here, please—where I can see all of you."

The words "all of you" set off alarm bells. Was it my weight that he was referring to? I glanced around for any sign of Isabella. When I didn't see her, I looked back at the man. "Are you here for the book signing?"

"Sort of." He tilted his head back and forth. "Is there a reason why you are hiding yourself behind that table?"

"I'm not hiding."

"Then step out here." He tapped one foot on the floor in front of him.

I narrowed my eyes. Who did this man think he was

to order me around? I didn't want to cause a commotion. I decided there could be no harm in stepping away from the table, but I did keep a good distance from the spot he'd touched on the floor.

"What can I do for you?" I frowned.

"I have to say that I'm a little disappointed." He tapped his chin.

"I'm sorry?"

"You should be." He sighed so hard that his shoulders drooped.

My eyes widened. "What are you talking about? Have I done something to upset you?"

"In your books you present yourself as this confident force of nature, but here I see you hiding behind a table, hesitant to present yourself to me. I might have made a mistake."

"Why would I present myself to you?" I raised an eyebrow. "Who are you?"

"Alistair Gordon." He held out a hand to me.

I took it in a quick shake that I hoped disguised the sweat on my palm. I recalled his name from dinner with Isabella. He was the designer.

"I'm sorry, Mr. Gordon, I didn't realize who you were."

"I didn't want you to. I thought it might make you nervous." He studied me as he took a few steps closer to me.

I held my breath as I endured the inspection.

"I guess you're just the nervous type. Which does disappoint me, I'll admit."

I bit into my bottom lip. It was a shining moment and I was dim. "I didn't expect you to be here this early." I cleared my throat. "The dress you designed is beautiful."

"No, it isn't." He scowled. "The dress is a rag. It's nothing. What matters is the woman who wears it. Now it will likely be a flop."

"There's no need to be mean." I crossed my arms.

"Isn't there? From your books you come across as a groundbreaker—a troublemaker—but what I see before me is a shrinking violet. What happened?" He stared into my eyes.

"I just was surprised about the fashion show. I aspire to be many things, but I've never claimed to have accomplished all of them." I shifted from one foot to the other. "I've been struggling a little lately. I won't lie about it. If you have time to find another model, it would probably be a good idea."

"Really?" He placed his hands on his hips. "That's your response?"

"I'm not sure what else I can say."

"You can tell me that you will wear that dress and make me even wealthier than I am. You can tell me that you are exactly who I expected you to be, and that you will prove it on the runway." He took a final step toward me and ended up so close that I could smell his cologne. "You might think that you are not the woman I want, but you are. I just need you to let that woman out."

"Okay. I'll try." I inched away from him.

CHAPTER 13

"Samantha, don't try—do." Alistair snapped his fingers right in front of my face.

A surge of annoyance rushed through me. Rude behavior always got under my skin.

"I am only who I am." I frowned. "That's all I can be."

"That's exactly who I want you to be. When you are on the runway today, I want to see you. If I don't, then no one will buy that dress. I promise you that. Many women can wear a dress, but only a few can bring it to life. That is what I need from you. This dress will enliven the hearts and minds of women across the world. Do you understand that, Samantha?"

"Yes, that's why I'm terrified." I blinked a few times to hide the tears that were building in my eyes. "I'm not sure that I'm qualified to do something like that."

"You don't need to be qualified, you just need to be you. It's not as if I'm asking for a miracle. You already are who you are, Samantha. You just need to figure out why you're hiding." He rapped his knuckles against my forehead in a light but annoying touch. "Come out to play, Samantha…please?"

"Wonderful, you've met Alistair." Isabella walked up to the table just as Alistair lowered his hand.

"Yes." I swallowed back unkind words. "Yes, he found me."

"I did." He turned to face Isabella. "Don't you look stunning? Not that I should be surprised. Ah, my beautiful creation." He stroked her cheek.

"Yes, it's true." Isabella laughed and kissed his cheek. "I suppose I should tell you, Samantha—Alistair took me out of horrible polyester pants suits and helped me to find my inner style. He's a very talented man, with an amazing eye for beauty. That's why it was no surprise to me when he wanted you for the show."

I lowered my eyes. So Alistair was all he claimed to be, yet I disappointed him.

"Yes. I'm sure she will do well." Alistair nodded at me. "See you soon, Samantha."

I smiled in return.

As he walked away, Isabella looked in my direction. "Samantha, you look pale? Are you sure you're not sick?"

"I'm not. I just can't place it. Something is off." I shook my head.

"Could you be…?" She pointed to my stomach.

"Hungry?" I shook my head.

"No, ah—I mean—sometimes women experience tiredness and lack of appetite in the first few weeks of pregnancy." Her smile grew wide.

"What?" My eyes spread wide. "No, absolutely not—not a chance. I'm not pregnant."

"Oh dear, I'm sorry. I overstepped. I didn't mean anything by it. I just didn't want you to feel you needed to hide it if it were true." Her cheeks flushed. "I'm so sorry. I hope I didn't upset you."

"No, you just startled me." I laughed. "I haven't even thought about pregnancy, and the idea that I might be kind of shocked me. I can assure you, pregnancy is not the problem."

"Then what is?" She took my hand. "I can be a good listener."

"I'm sure you can be, but people are beginning to arrive. We should get the signing started."

"Okay, but if you need to talk, I'm here, Samantha. I hope that you can think of me as your friend."

"Thank you, Isabella."

As the guests filed in and began to take their seats, I tried to push down the butterflies in my stomach. It occurred to me that I was completely disconnected from my body. I spent so much time learning to be in tune with it, and somehow all of that knowledge had disappeared. Sweat beaded on my forehead. My fingers fluttered against the sides of my pants.

I closed my eyes and willed myself to find my center. It wasn't too long ago that I didn't even have to look for it. Yet in front of this group of people my thoughts spun so fast that I couldn't even think of a greeting.

Isabella stepped up beside me.

"Welcome, everyone. Thank you for understanding our sudden change of venue. It is such a wonderful opportunity for us to have Samantha Bradford here. I know that she's looking forward to sharing her insights with all of us. So I'll just turn things over to her. Samantha." She smiled at me.

The audience applauded.

I smiled hard, in an attempt not to lose the muffin I'd eaten while ago. My heart jumped, then slammed hard against my chest. All eyes were on me. My lips parted and words began to form. I had no idea what I was saying until I heard it for myself.

"Thank you all for being here. I appreciate your support and hope that you can find a little inspiration from this reading." I turned to the pre-selected page from my book *Becoming Zara* and began to read. As the words flowed, I actually listened to them. I heard my own voice break through the text before me. The passion, the determination, and the inspiration filled more than just my audience—it filled me as well.

Yes, there was the Sammy that Max had been referring to. There was the Sammy that I'd been only a few days before.

When I closed the book and looked out at the audience, I saw a sea of faces. Each one was a little different than the others. It touched me to the core to think that despite their different walks of life, despite being on entirely different paths, they were all gathered together before me because of the book—because they'd found some truth in it, some inspiration in it. Who was I to doubt them?

As soon as Isabella announced the question and answer portion of the event, hands flew up into the air.

CHAPTER 14

I selected the first woman that I noticed with her hand raised.

"Yes, what is your question?"

She stood up and clutched her purse nervously. "Hello. It's so nice to see you in person. I hope you don't take offense at this question, but I really need to know."

"Please feel free to ask me anything that's on your mind." I smiled.

"In your book, you make it sound so easy. Zara is so good at everything. Even if she struggles at first she accomplishes all that she sets out to do. Do you think that's very realistic?" She glanced around at the other people in the audience. A few of the other women were nodding their heads as she spoke.

"I understand exactly what you mean. I think that if you were able to meet Zara, you'd see that she's pretty much just like you and me. We have our good days, and we have our bad days. The important thing is that on our bad days, we focus on our next good day. We remind ourselves that it's okay to have ups and downs—that it's just part of how we change and grow."

"That's an interesting point." The woman smiled. "Thank you." She sat back down in her chair.

I called on the next person I saw with her hand up.

"Yes, do you have a question?"

"I heard a rumor that this will be an ongoing series. Is that true? Are you afraid that you'll run out of material?" She looked me in the eye.

I took a breath and laughed a little. "I doubt that I'll ever run out of material. Yes, *Becoming Zara* is the lead-in to my new series called the *B.I.G. Girls Club*. It's a bit early to know for sure how long it will be, but I write a lot from my own experiences in life. As long as I'm still experiencing, I can assure you that I'll have material."

"Great. I'm looking forward to reading everything I can get my hands on." She sat back down in her chair.

I pointed to a young man who had his hand raised.

"Hi, Samantha. I follow your blog."

"Oh, wonderful. Thank you."

"Yes, it's great. But I was wondering if you feel that the blog is too personal? I find it difficult to be that open and honest with people in my life. I want to be, but that fear of being mocked is always there. How do you deal with that?"

His voice was gentle, but his question hit me hard. It reflected my emotions.

"To be honest with you, I don't always handle it well. I handle it better than I used to. But it is easy to slip into old habits. The thing about daring to trust life is that there are risks. I might make a mistake. I might just fall on my face. But at least I will have made the attempt. A fall is usually just an opportunity to get back up. A failure is a chance to learn and grow—to be more successful the next time. If we take our disappointments in stride, we'll never miss out on new opportunities."

"What an awesome perspective. I guess I'll keep on trying." He sat back down in his chair.

After a few more questions, the session ended.

I sat down at the table to sign books for each of the attendants. It occurred to me, as I scribbled my name and a short message on the front flap of each book, that I'd forgotten all about Max not being there once the book signing had started.

When I was down to the last book, I looked up to find Alistair right in front of me.

"You still want me to sign a book?" The pen hovered over the flap.

"Yes, very much. I enjoyed your reading and the question and answer session. I saw the woman I'd hoped to meet when you were speaking to people who needed you." He pushed the book closer to me. "Please sign it. I'm sure you will go on to write many other great works."

"Thank you." I jotted my signature and a short note to him about the difference he'd made in the lives of women with his bold fashion. When I handed the book back to him, he caught my hand between the cover and his palm for a moment.

"Are you going to bring that person on to the runway for me, Samantha?"

"Yes, sir." I smiled at him.

As he walked away, my heart fluttered. Could I really? It was one thing to speak to a group of people who already admired my work; it was quite another to pretend to be a model in front of people who were accustomed to actual models.

I spent a little time mingling with fans under Isabella's watchful eye. When the room finally cleared, she walked over to me.

"That was such a success. Would you be willing to do one more book signing the day after tomorrow?"

"Of course, anything you need. Do you think it went well?" I looked around at the last few people walking out of the room.

"Oh, absolutely. I think it's so refreshing that not only is your book amazing, you really are able to deliver that same inspiration in person." She shook her head. "I only wish I could bottle you."

"That might be difficult." I laughed. "But thank you. It's funny, before I started the session I was a mess, but once it started everything changed."

"It's easy to get caught up in the drama of day-to-day life. Let it roll off your back. We have to get you to the dressing room!" She tugged me down a short hallway that led to another section of the building.

If I thought the book signing was packed, the amount of people present in the next room was overwhelming. Wall-to-wall well-dressed people were gathered there.

"Oh, no! No, I don't think so." I started to back away.

Isabella stuck her hand firmly against my lower back and guided me forward. "You'll be fine. Remember? Once you get up there, you'll be great!"

CHAPTER 15

Isabella's words echoed through my mind, but my eyes blurred at the sight of the runway. She rushed me behind a curtain to a makeshift dressing room. In the small space there were six models. Each one was more slender and more perfect than the last. Was I really supposed to walk with these women? My dress might as well have been an elephant costume compared to what these women were wearing.

In the flurry of the preparations none seemed very friendly.

"Here's your dress." Isabella pointed to where it hung beside a tall mirror. "Daniella said the alterations will be perfect."

I recalled Daniella's lament about wardrobe malfunctions. How was I going to face the possibility that I might end up naked on the runway?

My eyes blurred for a different reason. Tears. Where was Max? I needed him to be there with me. I needed his easy smile and his perpetually supportive advice. I grasped my phone, prepared to call him, but before I could, Sue stepped up beside me.

"Let's go. We have to get you in your dress. You're the third one up"

"I'm what? Third? Why?" I could barely speak, as my breath was so short.

"Sh, just put on your dress." Sue waved her hand at me.

I noticed her left hand was tucked away as usual. The memory of her stories about bullying was a slap to my senses. Here was a woman who had overcome her insecurity about a birth defect, and I was worried about chubby thighs. How was I being an example to her? If I didn't think I could walk the runway, how could she believe that she should be able to display her unique hand proudly?

"Okay—yes, I'll put it on." I grabbed the dress and attempted to pull it off the hanger. The feat was quite a struggle. I became so frustrated that I almost tore one of the straps.

"Here, let me." Sue reached up with her left hand and was able to wriggle the sleeves off of the hanger. "It was stuck."

"Good thing you were here to help me." I shook my head. "Really, I'm not always this much of a mess."

"Oh, you're not a mess, Samantha. It's okay to be nervous. But there's no time to waste, so get changed. And remember, try not to fall off the stage." She laughed.

I didn't. She meant the warning as a joke, but that was

my worst fear.

I looked back at the gaggle of models. They didn't hesitate to reveal their flawless bodies. Could I really change in front of them? I tugged a section of the curtain forward in an attempt to give myself a bit more privacy.

In the middle of changing, I heard a shriek, followed by several other shrieks. The curtain whipped back. Only then did I realize that when I'd pulled the curtain, I'd also revealed a few of the models who were changing. My cheeks burned hot.

"How did that happen?" The tallest model huffed. "Who is in charge here?"

"Relax, Alia, it wasn't that bad. I'm sure no one saw more than what we usually show off on the runway." The woman beside her patted her back. "Try not to let it bother you." She looked around Alia to me.

I inched the skirt down over my thighs and looked away.

"That's easy for you to say, Priscilla. You're gorgeous. Why would you care if anyone saw you? But you know how wide my back is. It's horrible. I might as well be a man. The clothes hide that." Alia sniffled.

I couldn't help but eavesdrop. I was only a few feet away. Despite the fact that these women had absolutely nothing to hide, some seemed to be just as anxious at the thought of being exposed. I finished adjusting my dress and then walked over to the hair and make-up area. As a few of the models settled in beside me, I tried to keep my eyes straight ahead on the mirror. What must they think of me?

"You must be the special model Alistair mentioned. Samantha, is it?" Alia looked over at me as I nodded. "He's never done this before, you know."

"Maybe he shouldn't have at all." Priscilla shook her head. "You look terrified."

"I'll be fine when it's over."

"That's what I tell myself every time." Alia laughed. "Priscilla told me it would get easier each time, but so far that hasn't turned out to be true."

"You have to learn how to relax, Alia. Once you stop caring what the audience thinks, you'll own the runway." She looked into the mirror at my reflection. "If they sense fear, they'll eat you alive."

"Oh please, Priscilla, don't you think you're being a little dramatic?" Alia rolled her eyes.

One of the stylists ran her fingers through my hair. She spritzed it, fluffed it, then spritzed it again. Somehow those simple actions transformed my hair into a windswept look.

"I don't think I'm being dramatic at all. It's the truth." Priscilla dipped her head down as the stylist behind her wrapped her hair up in a tight bun.

"But the audience is who we have to impress. How can we not want them to like us?" Alia sighed.

"Trust me, you have to go out there with the intention that you will tell them what they will like. If you can do that, then you will dominate the runway." She lifted her head back up and looked at me. "Do you think that you can do that, Samantha?"

I stared at my windswept hair. The stylist spun me around and stroked my cheeks with blush. She accented my eyes with eyeliner and mascara.

"Maybe." I took a deep breath before the stylist set to work on my lips.

CHAPTER 16

By the time my make-up was finished, my heart was fluttering with fear. I gripped my phone again. Should I call him? Should I ask him to come—beg him to come? The lights went dim.

Alia grabbed my hand. "It's almost time."

"Don't fall, don't fall." I whispered the command to myself as I took my position in the line of women that would walk the short runway. At least it wasn't as long as a regular runway. I had less time to fall.

When the woman in front of me began to walk, my heart dropped.

Alia gave me a light push from behind. "It's your turn. You have to go now or you'll throw off the entire flow."

One foot in front of the other, Samantha, one foot in front of the other. Just do not fall! I kept my eyes trained on the audience. I heard the music, I saw the flash of the lights, but I did my best not to be swayed by it. When I reached the end of the runway, I mimicked the slight lunge and spin of the women who'd gone before me. At least I didn't fall.

I walked back toward the curtain. As I walked, I saw a look of horror in Alia's eyes when she looked at me. The expression made my skin crawl. Before I could figure out why she was looking at me in such a way, the ground disappeared.

In an attempt to make plenty of room for Alia, I'd walked dangerously close to the edge of the stage. Then my right foot walked right off it. I tumbled to the ground beside the runway—well, my body did. My head landed in the lap of a man who looked very frightened.

"I'm so sorry." I looked up at him as I lifted my head from his lap.

Isabella rushed toward me. "Are you okay? Did you twist your ankle?"

"I'm okay," I whispered. I couldn't look at her. I couldn't breathe. I couldn't think. If I did, the tears would start.

"Let me help you up."

As I stood up, I saw the other models—professional as ever—continue down the runway without incident.

Isabella led me back behind the curtain.

"Is the dress okay?" I looked it over in a daze. "I didn't tear it, did I?"

"It's fine. What matters is that you're okay. Are you?" She searched my eyes.

"I think so—other than being mortified. I knew this was a terrible idea."

"Which is exactly why this happened." Alistair stood just behind the curtain and stared at me. "That fear is what made you make a mistake."

"Or maybe it was because I've never walked this runway before. I was distracted by all the commotion, and I forgot that I needed to keep both feet on the runway. Isn't that possible?" I looked at him helplessly. "I'm sorry about your show, but I'm just not cut out for this."

"I disagree. I expect you to be here tonight for the show. It was part of our agreement. Can I count on you to be there?" He met my eyes.

Isabella grimaced as she looked over at me.

If I didn't show, it might cause her some serious trouble.

"Alistair, do you really want me there? After what happened today?"

"Yes, I do. I expect you to be there. A moment is just a moment, after all. What happens tonight may just be fabulous." He smiled. "If you want it to be, that is." He winked at me.

When he walked away I thought about calling out to stop him. It would be best to let him know that I was not going to be there—to tell him while he still had time to replace me in the show. By the time I looked up, he was already out the door.

Isabella rubbed her hand along my back. "It's really not so bad, Samantha. Falls happen all the time. You're not the first and you won't be the last."

"It's not just that, Isabella. I'm all about stepping outside of my comfort zone, but maybe I've stepped out too far this time. I'm in over my head, and the last thing I want to do is draw ridicule to Alistair." I sighed and looked away. "Maybe this is all just too much."

"I find that hard to believe. I know I don't know you that well, Samantha, but to me it feels like we share many traits. I can tell you that never once did I doubt that you'd be able to handle all this. Maybe it's you that needs to have more faith in yourself?"

"Maybe. I can't believe Alistair still wants me in the show."

"Just do the best you can. Let this incident roll off your back. Things happen in life. If we don't dwell on them, they can't control us. Let me know if there's anything I can do." She gave my hand a light shake. "You'll do well."

"Thanks, Isabella." My smile was genuine, but I wished I could believe her. She spoke every word that I, myself, might have spoken to a friend, but they failed to cross through the dark cloud that was hanging over me. I couldn't recall a time when I felt more lost.

As confusion overwhelmed me, I pulled out my phone to call Max. He didn't answer so I waited for his voicemail.

"Max, you really should have been here." I pressed the phone against my ear. "I needed you."

Just as I hung up I heard his voice.

CHAPTER 17

"I was here, Sammy. I saw everything." Max walked over to me.

Relief flooded me. At least he hadn't truly abandoned me. Maybe his presence in the audience meant that I hadn't been alone.

"I'm sorry that happened."

"I told you—I told all of you, but no one believed me." I lowered my eyes to hide the tears that threatened to fall.

"Hey, it's okay." He wrapped his arm around my shoulders. "You fell. It's not the first time."

"Thanks for the reminder." I laughed and wiped at my eyes. "That just makes my point even more clear. I knew this was a risk, I knew that there was a good chance I'd end up making a fool of myself, and instead of trusting my instincts, I listened to everyone else."

"Did you know it, or did you make it happen?" He sat down next to me.

"Max! Of course I didn't make this happen. You

think I enjoy feeling mortified? I may not be perfectly balanced, but I certainly wouldn't do that to myself."

He took my hand and gave it a squeeze. "I don't mean on purpose. I just mean, maybe if you weren't so nervous it wouldn't have happened. In case you haven't noticed, most of your accidents happen when you're feeling anxious."

I never treasured a hand more than his in that moment. I clung to it as if it could keep me afloat even though we weren't in the water.

"Max. What is wrong with me?" I looked into his eyes. "Can you tell me?"

"Nothing is wrong with you, Sammy. You're perfect just the way you are." He trailed his fingertips along my cheek. "I'm not sure what has you so rattled, but I know that if you take the time to think about it, you'll be able to figure it out. Let's go back to the hotel for a bit."

"Oh, I don't think I can come back and do this again tonight." I closed my eyes. "In fact, I don't want to."

"Sammy, you don't give up on things." He caught my chin with a light squeeze. "You're going to make it through this. Let's just go back to the hotel. You can have a nice bath and I'll give you a massage."

"Wow, you're right." I stared at him.

"I know, it's rare." He grinned. "Remember?"

"No, I mean you're right that I depend on you. You're so ready to pamper me, when I should be able to handle this myself." I shook my head. "I never realized what a position I put you in."

"I don't mind. I love taking care of you. I just don't like to see you struggle." He sighed and rested his forehead against mine. "I want the whole world to be perfect for you, so maybe I'm guilty of trying to protect you too much. You'll find your footing, Sammy."

"Not if I hide out in the hotel." I stood up, with his hand still in mine. "I want to go out into the city. Let's go have some lunch. I want to do the opposite of everything that I have been doing lately. Maybe that will clear my head a bit."

"Sounds great." He led me toward the door. "I'll be here tonight, you know."

"It wasn't your fault, Max. I shouldn't have said that. Whatever is making me stumble is all on me." I kissed his cheek. "But I am sure glad I have you here to help me figure it out."

"Motorbike?" He pulled the keys from his pocket.

"Absolutely."

As I hugged him tight and the world flew by, I realized that it wasn't just my body I wasn't satisfied with. A part of me still seemed to be waiting for Max to reject me. Despite how clear and forthcoming he'd been about his feelings, I still expected him to come to his senses and walk away.

If he knew that I was even thinking such things, he'd be upset. He had a right to be. It showed a lack of trust that I thought I'd left behind long ago.

Why was I so very twisted up inside? Why did it seem like the lightest breeze could send me spiraling off my path? If there was ever going to be a moment that I should declare happiness as my fulltime state of mind, wouldn't Venice in Max's arms be one of those moments?

Max eased the motorbike to a stop outside a small cafe.

"I'm starving." He wrapped his arm around my waist as we walked inside. "I can't wait to see the menu."

"I don't even need a menu. I know exactly what I want." I grinned.

He pulled out a chair for me.

As I sat down, I reminded myself how lucky I was to be with him. For so long I thought it would never happen, but there he was—right across from me, his gaze locked to mine.

"What's it going to be?"

"Chicken Alfredo. How could I pass it up?"

I sensed relief in his smile as he nodded. "Good. The last thing you want to do is miss out on the good food in Italy."

Once we placed our order I did my best to make conversation. I tried to keep a positive tone, and even pointed out how lucky we were to be in Venice. It all would have been true, if I could only just let the thoughts go about my fall from the runway.

Max was right. It certainly hadn't been the first time that it had happened to me, but it was probably the most public of any mishaps I'd had. How could I manage it again that night?

When the chicken Alfredo arrived, I dug in and even tried a bite of Max's ravioli. I enjoyed indulging in one of my favorite meals, and though I'd had many delicious dishes, this by far outshined them all.

"Wow, I might never be able to go back home. I'll miss the food!"

"That'll give us a good reason to come back." Max smiled.

"Do you think we will? This seems like such a once-in-a-lifetime kind of thing, doesn't it?"

"Samantha, if your book keeps doing so well and your next follows suit, you're going to have the freedom to go anywhere and do anything you want." Max took a bite of my Alfredo. "You shouldn't limit yourself."

"Hm." I finished my food as I thought about his words.

Was that the problem? Was I limiting the amount of success I was allowing myself?

CHAPTER 18

When we left the restaurant, the uneasiness followed me. I wanted to think my way out of the problem I faced, when what I really needed to do was feel my way out.

"Can we do a little window shopping?" I pointed to the slew of tiny shops not far from the restaurant.

"Sure." Max hooked his arm through mine.

As I perused the assortment of goods, I found that delicate items drew my attention—tiny figurines, little glass shoes, and even dainty teacups. None of these things were my usual style. Could it be that my own sense of fragility was reflected in these items?

By the time we left the shops, it was close to time for the fashion show. My stomach filled with nerves as the time ticked by. I managed to eat a light salad, while I paced back and forth.

"Samantha, you're going to wear yourself out before you get on the runway." Max laughed.

"Please don't say that. The last thing I need is another runway disaster."

"Don't predict it, just let it happen. I'm going to be

there with you." He took my hand. "Every step of the way."

"Thank you, Max. I appreciate it."

"Just try all of your usual methods—meditation, yoga, deep breathing, maybe something playful. You have to get out of your head."

"I know, I know. But I don't have any time for that." I glanced at my watch. "I need to head out right now, actually."

"You can do this, Sammy, I know you can." He leaned in for a kiss.

Even his kiss, which at one time not long ago would have had me in a puddle on the floor, struck me in that moment as a waste of time. I didn't want to be late. I didn't want to make things worse than they already were.

"I have to get my things." I jumped up to gather my purse and a bottle of water, then we were off to the show.

In the car on the way there, Max tried to engage me a few times in conversation, but I couldn't think or speak. I could only envision a perfect walk down the runway. It was time to redeem myself. If I kept my mind focused, I believed that I could do just that.

Confidence flooded through me until we walked into the venue. It was much larger than the one I'd been in earlier that day. Also, this runway was twice as long. The people in the audience were just as fancy. I noticed the man whose lap I'd landed in sat a few rows back from the front.

I took a deep breath and kissed Max on the cheek. "I'd better just bite the bullet and get back there."

"Hey." He looked into my eyes. "It's supposed to be fun, remember?"

I laughed and shook my head as I walked away from him. His words were an attempt at brightening my mood, but they couldn't be further from the truth. The only fun I looked forward to was when the show was over.

When I walked into the dressing room I expected to hear laughter or maybe even a few mocking comments. Surely after my fall on the runway the professional models would have a few things to say about me.

Instead, when I stepped inside, I was greeted by a light round of applause. My cheeks grew hot as I thought they were teasing me.

"I know, I know—it was horrible."

"No!" Alia jumped up. "Not at all. You handled it really well, and you're back tonight. That's amazing!"

"It doesn't surprise me." Priscilla looked over at me. "I knew she was tough from the first moment I saw her. It takes a strong woman to endure that kind of stumble and then show her face again."

"Well, I have an obligation."

"But it's more than that, isn't it?" Alia stood up and walked over to me. "I've fallen twice since I started modeling. The first time I didn't get back on the runway for a month. The second time I nearly quit modeling altogether."

"Why?" I looked at her with wide eyes. "You're an amazing model. Why would you want to give that up?"

"I didn't want to, but I was sure no one would be able to forget. I figured I'd never do well, so I should just give up." She looked over at Priscilla. "It was Priscilla who talked me out of it. She told me that if I wanted something bad enough, a million falls—a million embarrassing moments—wouldn't keep me from getting back on the runway. She was right and here you are, so you must have a pretty powerful passion for something too."

"It's true." Priscilla nodded. "It's all about what you want. That's why I can leave it all on the runway. If it was a good walk, great. If it was not so good—oh well, there will be another walk. We're here to do a job and that job doesn't have to be difficult unless we make it so."

"Very good point." I leaned against the wall and looked at all of the gorgeous dresses lined up.

I could recall a time when I'd refused to even walk inside stores because I guessed that all of their beautiful dresses would not be in my size. Alistair could change that. He was changing that. He wanted to create glamorous dresses in all shapes and sizes. That was certainly something to be passionate about.

Not only was I enamored by the idea of Alistair's creations, I was impressed by the advice given to me by the two models I'd gotten to know. It was easy to look at a beautiful woman and assume she had no insecurities, but that wasn't the truth—not at all.

Alia and Priscilla both had their own beliefs about their bodies, as did the rest of the women I'd overheard in the dressing room. Some had ankles that were too thick in their opinion; others had elbows that jutted out too harshly.

If women who were held up as the ideals of beauty couldn't find a way to embrace their bodies, then what chance was there for the average woman?

That's where I came in. My opportunity to represent the average woman was more powerful than I'd even first realized.

I eased my way into my dress, smoothed it down and accepted the attention of the stylist.

When we lined up for the final walk my heart fluttered. This was it. Was I going to fall again? Was I going to end up in some other poor sap's lap?

CHAPTER 19

I reminded myself that Max was there. Somewhere in the sea of faces his smile waited to greet me.

With slow even breaths I watched each of the girls before me walk out onto the runway. As each one returned without any stumbles or nosedives I reminded myself that it could be done. Then it was my turn.

I blanketed myself in the passion I had for the dress I wore and the cause it supported. Even if I couldn't be confident, I could be proud.

With long even strides I made my way down to the end of the runway. At the end, I placed one hand on my hip, swirled my body around, and began to walk back. As I did, another model approached me. It struck me that earlier in the day I'd moved to the edge of the runway, not because there wasn't enough room, but out of habit. I often gave plenty of room to people around me, as if I were a mountain rather than a woman.

I forced myself to stay on the same path. We didn't come close to touching.

When I made it behind the curtain I nearly collapsed

with relief. Applause from the audience let me know that the show had come to an end.

It was over. I'd done it. My heart still pounded as if it might burst, but I'd done it. A thin sheen of sweat covered my skin.

"Samantha."

Alistair's voice drew my attention. Was he pleased? Was he upset?

I looked into his eyes as he walked up to me.

"Thank you. Thank you for being present on the runway tonight. I've already received several amazing responses to the dress. As a gift, I'd like for you to keep it. I couldn't imagine it being on anyone else." He looked over the dress and then back up at me. "You gave it life."

"Thank you, Alistair. At first I was a little upset about doing this, but now I'm very grateful for the opportunity."

"I'm glad." He gave my hand a firm shake. "Any time you are back in Venice let me know. I'd love to get you on the runway again."

I smiled as he walked away, yet the very thought still filled me with horror.

"Hey, beautiful!" Max's arms wrapped around me from behind. "You were breathtaking. Just like I knew you would be."

"Thanks, Max." I turned in his arms to look into his eyes.

"Were you able to get centered? You sure seemed to

be."

"No." I sighed. "Not really. I was able to cover it up, but I was still terrified. I really need to figure out what has me so frazzled."

"Should we take a walk along the water and talk about it?" Max slipped his hand into mine.

"I don't know. Do we have time for that?" My heart lurched anxiously.

"Sammy, we don't have any other plans for two days. We have plenty of time. We can try the gondola ride again. Plus, I have something special planned for us tomorrow." He stroked the back of my hand. "We can slow down a little bit and really enjoy our time here."

His words sunk deep into my thoughts. "That's it! Time. I've been so rushed since we left France. I didn't take the time to do any meditation—no yoga, no blogging, no nothing. I've lost my center because I'm not making time to find it."

"That sounds about right." Max exhaled. "We have been on a pretty tight schedule."

"But not too tight for five minutes of meditation or a little activity. That's just an excuse. I've fallen back into the idea that I have to prove my worth in order to be here. So, instead of taking care of myself, I've spent all my time stressing out. Wow, how did I lose track so easily?" I slid my arm through his as we walked out of the building. "I'm sorry, Max. I've been relying on you way too much and not even recognizing how much support you've been giving me."

"That's what I'm here for, Sammy."

As we reached the parking lot I noticed Isabella waving at me from the front of the building.

"Oh, wait just a second, Max. Isabella must need something."

"I'll be right here." He leaned back against the car that was waited for us.

Isabella met me halfway. "You did a great job, Samantha. Thank you so much. We're still on for the next book signing, right?"

"Yes, absolutely."

"Great. I really saw your determination out on the runway. You handled it very well."

"Alistair let me keep the dress." I did a quick spin. "What do you think?"

"Gorgeous. Maybe a bit too dressy for the book signing, though."

"Don't worry, I'll wear something more casual for it."

"Do you two have any plans for tomorrow?" She looked past me in Max's direction.

"Max said he has something special planned. Plus, I think I'm going to take some time to get back to basics. I've been so busy that I've been neglecting some things I need to do for myself."

"If you're interested, there's a full circle meditation in the morning. It happens at sunrise and it's a beautiful experience. I'll text you the address just in case." She looked up at the sky. "As long as the weather is good, we'll be out there."

"Thanks, Isabella. I'll do my best to make it."

"Enjoy your night." Isabella waved to Max, then turned back toward the building.

As I joined Max beside the car he looked into my eyes. "What was that about? More fashion shows?"

"No, she invited me to a sunrise meditation." I smiled. "It sounds beautiful."

"Sunrise? Like when the sun comes up?" Max quirked a brow. "Isn't that a little early?"

"It'll be refreshing."

He opened the door to the car for me. "Okay, but do you mind if it's refreshing alone? I really don't have any interest in getting up that early tomorrow."

"Sure, that's fine. It won't interfere with your plans, will it?" I settled in the car.

"Not at all." He closed the door behind me.

Once Max climbed in the other side, the driver headed toward the hotel.

Max interlaced his fingers with mine. "I'm really looking forward to having some time alone with you, Sammy."

"I am too." I leaned close, then looked out the window.

I looked forward to my time with Max, but I looked forward to my time with me too. I wanted to get back on track with my spiritual and emotional journey. I couldn't exactly advise other women to take time for themselves if I wasn't able to allow myself to do the same thing.

CHAPTER 20

Max and I arrived at the hotel restaurant just in time to land a perfect table.

"You know what I want?" I grinned.

"Chicken Alfredo?" He raised an eyebrow.

"Always—but something else."

"What?"

"Pizza!"

"Oh, great idea." He gestured to the waiter. "Do you serve pizza?"

The waiter stuck his nose in the air. "This may be hard to believe, sir, but every restaurant in Italy does not serve pizza. This would be one that does not."

"Oh." Max frowned. "I guess we could go somewhere else." He looked over at me.

"No, it's fine, I'm sure we can get pizza another time. I'll order something else."

The waiter left menus on the table for us to look at.

I ordered a salad and pasta combination. Max ordered spaghetti and meatballs. I didn't think Italy was going to be doing any favors for my waistline.

I picked at my food and shared a little conversation with Max, but my mind was focused on the day I'd had. Maybe it had ended in success, but I'd still experienced an extreme sense of unease. More than anything, I wanted to get back to that confident woman that I thought I'd become.

"Sammy, you're a million miles away. You okay?"

"I think so. There's something off. I just can't put my finger on it."

"Maybe some down time in the room will help."

"Maybe." I nodded.

After we finished our meals Max offered dessert. "Maybe something covered in chocolate sauce?"

"I'd better not. I've eaten enough pasta today to grow a pasta tree."

"A pasta tree?" He grinned. "I don't think pasta grows on trees."

"Maybe not, but if I eat any more, I guarantee you, there could be a pasta tree."

"I'd like to see a pasta tree. Do you think you could climb it?"

I sighed. "Of course not. It would be too floppy."

"But pasta is hard before you cook it." He wagged his finger at me.

"But it's brittle."

"Good point. I give, you win."

"You just want to get me back to the hotel room." I

winked at him.

"It's true, I do." He paid the bill and we headed for the elevator.

The moment I set foot inside the suite my nerves settled a little. It was good to be alone with Max. It was good not to feel under pressure to perform at a book signing or a fashion show. But still, something prickled at my mind.

Max and I snuggled up and watched a movie together. It was much-needed quiet time—time for just the two of us to hang out together, but just as he was about to slide closer to me on the couch I glanced at my watch.

"Sorry, hon, I really want to be up in time for that meditation. Do you mind if I turn in early?" I met his eyes in time to see a hint of disappointment.

"Of course. It's fine. I'm sure you're tired from today. Go on to bed. I'll be in soon." We shared a quick kiss.

I set my alarm on my phone to be sure that I'd be up in time the next morning. As I sprawled out in bed to really relax for the first time since I'd arrived in Venice, my heartbeat slowed. It was surprising to me that I was completely unaware of the amount of anxiety I'd been living with. If it was that easy for me to ignore my body's signals, then I had a lot of self-work yet to do. A good night's sleep might help with that.

I willed myself to fall asleep. I counted sheep. I tried some color visualization. I recited sleep-inducing affirmations. But when Max walked into the room, my eyes flew right open.

"Are you still up?" He crawled into bed beside me.

"Yes, I'm not sure why."

"Maybe you missed me?" He snuggled close and kissed my cheek.

"I definitely missed you. I'm having a hard time falling asleep. I can't figure out why."

"You've had a busy day. Want a massage?" He rubbed my shoulder.

"Oh yes, that would be perfect."

I rolled over onto my stomach. Max's hands kneaded deep into my muscles. With every roll of pressure I relaxed a little more. I closed my eyes and waited for sleep to envelop me. Instead, I experienced even more wakefulness.

Max stretched out beside me and yawned. "I'm looking forward to tomorrow."

"Me too." I curled close to him.

Maybe that was it? My longing for the excitement of the next day was preventing me from falling asleep?

As I mulled the possibilities over in my mind, I realized that my entire pattern was out of balance. I'd been sleeping a lot less and eating erratically. There hadn't been much of a routine to my life since I'd been on the tour. Maybe my body was crying out for a little more attention.

At some point, long after Max had begun to snore, I

fell asleep.

CHAPTER 21

When my alarm went off, it was a bit of a shock. I didn't want to wake up. I considered turning it off, but the draw of the sunrise meditation was enough to get me up out of bed. Hopefully being at a gathering of like-minded people would allow me to reconnect with my inner self.

I dressed as quietly as I could in an attempt not to wake Max.

When I slipped out the door my body ached with exhaustion. Without getting much sleep the night before, my stamina just wasn't there. Still, I rode the elevator down to the lobby, then hailed a taxi to take me to the address of the meditation.

The sun was just peeking over the horizon as I arrived. A small grassy park welcomed me. Toward the south end, a group of people sat in a wide circle. I noticed Isabella in the group, but she already had her eyes closed. I didn't want to disturb her. I found an open spot and sat down in it.

In the center of the circle a woman was playing

singing bowls. The sound soothed me in such a way that my entire mood lightened. I took a breath—a real breath, a deep fulfilling breath—then I released it. I expanded as my breath expelled from my body. The limitations of bone and skin blurred as if I were becoming a cloud that drifted just above the ground.

I closed my eyes and listened to the sound of the singing bowls. The vibration of the melody carried across my nerves, first plucking, then soothing each one. I savored the experience.

There it was—that peace that evaded me, that sense of place within the wide wonderful universe. I invited it to wash through every cell in my body. Lighter and lighter—even feeling slightly dizzy—I detached from all of the burdens I'd been collecting—the burden of anxiety, the burden of ego, the burden of expectations. Warmth spread throughout my body and for the first time in quite some time, a sense of wholeness flooded through me. I'd fought so hard to find the place I belonged, when the only place I truly belonged was within my own center. When I was there, the world molded itself around me.

A shiver coursed up along my spine. It was so powerful that my eyes sprang open in reaction to it. The sun broke through the clouds in that exact moment. It nearly blinded me with its golden hue. It was perfect.

As the meditation ended, a few people began to mingle. I tried to make my way over to Isabella, but other people seemed to be occupying her attention. While I waited, I pulled my shoes off and walked through the thick grass. Still a bit damp from the morning dew, it clung to my feet.

I thought back to how anxious and rushed I'd been lately. I'd lost all focus on myself because my mind had been occupied by my need to please others. In the process, I'd become such an anxious mess that I'd sabotaged my own success.

It made me sick to my stomach to think that I'd almost given up on everything. How could I lose clearness of sight so easily?

I took another belly-filing deep breath. Just as I released it, the stinging started. My eyes flew open. I looked down at my feet to see ants all over them.

"No!" I yelped and danced around in an attempt to avoid the ants.

Isabella noticed my distress and rushed over to check on me. "Are you dancing or are you hurt?" She grabbed my arm.

"Ants—ants everywhere!"

"Oh no—it should be out of season for those little bugs. Here, there's a bathroom over here." She pulled me toward a stone building.

Once inside, I thrust one of my feet into the sink. The cold water rushed over my foot and washed away the ants. I switched to the other foot and rinsed it off. The little ants swirled and went down the sink. I might have felt guilty for their fate if it weren't for the burning and itching of my feet.

"Some way to start the day." Isabella handed me some towels. "I'm sorry that this happened."

"It's okay. I had a great meditation. I guess I'll just have to be gentle to my feet." I smiled.

"I'll go grab your shoes."

As soon as Isabella left the bathroom I bent down and clawed at my feet. They itched worse than poison ivy. The more I scratched, the more they itched.

"Get a hold of yourself, Sammy, before you scratch your skin off." I sighed and stood up. My reflection in the mirror told me all I needed to know.

I might have been centered for a moment, but that moment had now disappeared.

CHAPTER 22

I met Isabella outside the bathroom. As I tugged on my shoes she assessed the state of the bites.

"If you get some cream you'll be fine. The itch doesn't last too long." She looked up at me and frowned. "You're not getting the best impression of Venice, I'm afraid."

"I have an adventurous day ahead of me. I'm looking forward to it." I leaned against the outside wall of the restroom and fastened the straps on my sandals. "I think I'll keep my shoes on, though."

"Yes, that might be best." Isabella walked with me to the parking lot. "Can I give you a ride back to the hotel?"

"Thanks, that would be great."

"It'll give us a chance to chat." She unlocked the doors to her car.

Something about her voice made me look over at her with some concern.

"Sure." I sat down in the passenger seat and buckled my seat belt.

As Isabella drove she described some of the locations that we passed. "Growing up here was magical, I can't deny it. It's not like any other place in the world." She pointed through the windshield at a crumbling structure. "That was once a little ice cream shop. They're putting in yet another restaurant. Like we need another." She laughed. "Ah well, the important thing is that people enjoy their visit."

"How could they not?" I smiled as I looked out the window.

"Are you?" Isabella looked over at me.

"I am."

"When I met you in France you seemed to be having the time of your life, but I've noticed that things are different since you've been here. I just hope it's nothing I've done. Maybe pushing you into the fashion show wasn't fair to you." She sighed and turned toward the hotel.

"No. Oh no, please don't think that. The fashion show is something I never would have done without a little push, and I think it was good for me. I just think that I'm a little caught up in the whirlwind of the tour. It's hard for me to figure out what's happening next when I'm constantly on the move. I didn't expect that to affect me this much."

"I suppose that would be difficult. I just hope that you're able to enjoy yourself a little before it's time for you to move on."

"I'm sure I will. I'm sorry if I've given you the impression that I'm not happy. You've done so much to make our stay here special. I really couldn't be happier with everything you've done."

"Well, maybe without the ant bites." Isabella laughed as she parked the car outside the hotel. "Have a great day, Samantha. If you need anything just let me know."

"Thanks, Isabella." I leaned across to give her a quick hug. "Please don't ever think that I don't appreciate everything that you've done for me. This has been one of the best experiences of my life. Just when I thought I couldn't be pushed any further, you showed me a new way to grow. I think I'm just having a few growing pains along the way."

"Perfect for the next book, right?" Isabella smiled.

"I hope so." I laughed and stepped out of the car.

I reached the lobby in time to meet Max as he stepped off the elevator.

"How did you know I was here?" I hugged him.

"I hoped. I thought that if you weren't, I might go out hunting for you." He looked into my eyes. "I missed you this morning."

"I'm sorry. I didn't want to wake you. I thought one of us should get some sleep."

"You didn't sleep well last night?" He narrowed his eyes. "I noticed a bit of tossing and turning."

"I just couldn't fall asleep. I tried, I really did." I stifled a yawn.

"Then maybe we should stay in today so you can get some sleep." He raised an eyebrow. "I don't want you to be exhausted for the book signing tomorrow."

"No way, I've been looking forward to this. I just need to pick up some cream for my feet."

He looked down at the numerous bug bites on my feet. "I see meditation in the park may not have gone so well?"

"It wasn't my best moment, but I'm sure the rest of the day will be great. I can't wait to find out what you have in store for me. Are you going to give me a clue?" I grinned as I looked into his eyes.

"It's going to be a very sweet experience." He winked.

"Hm. Sweet. Any time we spend the day together is sweet." I pecked his lips. "I guess we should hurry, we don't want to waste any time."

"Wait." He pulled me close. "That's what I don't want you to do."

"What do you mean?" I gazed into his eyes.

"I don't want you to hurry. I don't want you to think about the time. I just want you to be with me."

"I will be." I leaned into his arms. "Always."

"I know, but what I mean is, I want you to be present with me. I know you've got a lot on your mind, but I'd like you to try your best to let all that go. I just want one day where it's just you and me—no books, no tour, no worries—just us." He brushed his hand back through my hair and stroked the back of my neck. "What do you say?"

"I say that sounds like paradise." I kissed him again, then pulled away.

He pulled me back and kissed me again. Within moments I disappeared in the heady pleasure of his kiss. The sensation was one that I loved, but it also reminded me of how long I'd gone without it. Sure we'd been kissing, but not that deep soul-intertwining, outside-world-vanishing type of kissing. I lingered in the afterglow of it with his arms still wrapped around me.

"Max, I love you."

"I love you too, Sammy." He kissed the top of my head. "I love being here with you. I love that we're going to spend the day together."

"Doing what, exactly?" I looked up at him with a sneaky smile. "Are you going to tell me, or do I have to keep guessing?"

CHAPTER 23

"You can't stand it, can you?" Max raised an eyebrow.

"You know I'm not a fan of surprises." I stuck out my bottom lip.

"You mean you're not a fan of not being in control?" He smirked.

"Stop!" I laughed. "Please, just tell me."

"Alright, fine." He offered a dramatic sigh.

"We're going on a gelato tour."

"A what?" I narrowed my eyes.

"A gelato tour. See?" He held up a piece of paper. "Each of these shops offers an assortment of flavors and this little guide will take us through the most unique ones. So we get a chance to try as many flavors as we like."

I looked at the glossy paper. Each building had a picture of a scrumptious-looking gelato. My mouth watered at the sight of them, but my chest also tightened. They were full of sugar. How was that going to fit into my diet?

"Max." I frowned and looked up from the paper. "Do you really think that's a good idea?"

"Obviously I do, otherwise I wouldn't have suggested it. What's wrong with it?" The tension around his eyes indicated that he was disappointed in my reaction.

"I'm trying to lose weight, Max, not gain it." My entire body grew tense.

"And it doesn't always have to be about that, Sammy. Does it?" He shook his head. "We're in Italy, I want us to have a little fun. Is that so bad?"

"A little fun can mean a serious backslide." I glanced away from him for a moment and drew a deep breath. "I'm sorry, I know that you planned this as a special outing for us. I don't mean to be negative, but I just think that I need to get back in control of my diet—and everything else."

"There's that 'c' word again." He rolled his eyes. "What is the point of being in Italy together if we don't get to enjoy it?"

"There's nothing wrong with enjoying things, Max, but there's no need to give up all control to enjoy myself. I can have fun doing things that don't involve a day filled with dessert. There's nothing wrong with wanting to be in control, especially when things have been so chaotic." I rested a hand on his chest and looked into his eyes. "Why is it so bad that I want to hold on to that?"

"It's not bad, it's just exhausting. I think sometimes it's okay to lose a little control." He stepped closer to me and swept his arm around my back. "We are in Italy. Do I need to repeat that? We're in a part of the world that we might never have the chance to be in again. I don't want to leave here without you having the chance to relax and truly enjoy yourself." He curled his hands around mine and gave a firm squeeze. "I'm going to break you out of this apprehension you've been dealing with, if it takes me the entire tour."

I pulled my hands from his and set my jaw. After counting to three to calm myself down I settled my gaze on him.

"Maybe what you want isn't what's best, Max. You know that one of the biggest changes I've had to make in my life was removing food as a source of entertainment. I learned to have fun without food being a part of it. Now you're asking me to do something—"

"You make it sound as if I'm trying to get you to break the law." He folded his arms across his chest and turned his back to me. "I'm sorry. You're right. I guess I should have calculated the calorie content before I even thought about the idea. Then I could have faxed the results to Isabella to see if I had her approval, and I'm guessing the approval of the tour manager and—let's see, maybe even the publisher?" He glanced over his shoulder at me. "You don't belong to them, Samantha. Just because you're working for them, that doesn't mean that you have to mold yourself to be what you think everyone else wants you to be. But if that's what you want, then from now on, I'll make sure that we keep a running list of everything you put in your mouth. Do they need to know about our sex life too? Doesn't that count as exercise?"

My heart beat hard against my chest. The more he spoke, the harder it beat. "Max, that isn't fair." I locked my eyes onto his. "I've already splurged a lot. I'm just trying to make better choices for myself. If you can't support that—"

"Don't!" He lifted one finger in the air and turned fully to face me. "Don't tell me that I don't support you. I've supported you every step of the way. I've seen you deny yourself simple pleasures that everyone else gets to enjoy. I've seen you exercise when you should have been resting. I know what sacrifices you make, and I'm proud of you for them. But you can't always be sacrificing, Sammy, and neither can I."

"Is that what it feels like to you? That you're having to sacrifice to be with me?" Tears blurred my eyes as the weight of my lack of sleep rippled through my emotions.

"No Sammy, that's not what I said—not at all." He cupped my cheeks with his hands. "I treasure every moment I have with you. Just once in a while, I'd like to see that you're enjoying it too."

I blinked back the tears and sighed. "On the one day we have to spend together uninterrupted, we pick a fight with one another. I have let things get really out of balance. That's why I'm trying to get back to my routine. Can't you see that?"

CHAPTER 24

Max looked away from me for a moment. His shoulders rose and fell with a deep breath. When he looked back at me his expression was thoughtful.

"I'm sorry. You're right. I guess I just didn't think it through. I should have been more considerate. We can find something else to do. All I want is time with you, no matter what we're doing."

The strain in his voice made me swallow hard. Was I making everything about me? Was that the kind of marriage I wanted to have? After all, he was in Italy too.

"No, you know what? I'm the one that's wrong. You're right. This is supposed to be fun too. I like your idea. You know how much I love my sweets. Why don't we go on the tour, and I'll just take a taste of each of yours. By the time the tour is done, I'll have eaten about one gelato and gotten to sample all the flavors. If you're willing to share, that is." I poked him in the side.

"Oh, I'm willing." He smiled. I saw the light of excitement return in his eyes. "Are you sure you don't mind?"

"I don't mind, Max. I love that you thought of this. I am trying to relax and enjoy myself. I'm just having a hard time getting there." I stifled another yawn.

"We'll make it a quick tour. So you can get some extra sleep."

"I'm sorry, I just need some coffee." I hid another yawn.

"Alright, why don't you get some cream for your feet, I'll pick us up some coffees, and then we'll head out."

"Thanks, Max." I hugged him, then pulled back to look into his eyes. "I'm so glad we get to spend the day together."

I stopped in the shop in the lobby of the hotel and was able to find some cream for my feet. After I took a few minutes in a chair in the corner to coat them, I ducked into the bathroom to wash up.

"Have you seen the new line by Alistair?"

I overheard a conversation between two women at the sinks as I washed my hands.

"Yes, it's amazing. I can't believe that some of those high-end clothes are going to be available for regular women now. No more gazing at the magazines—we get to actually buy the dresses."

"Yes, if we can afford them." The other woman laughed.

I smiled to myself as they finished washing their hands. It was nice to see the fashion industry opening up to all women.

I joined Max in front of the hotel.

"Coffee." He handed me one.

I accepted it and blew into the top of the cup to cool it some.

"Perfect. I'll be in top shape in no time."

"How about we take that gondola ride first? It'll give us time to enjoy our coffee and keep you off your feet for a bit."

"That's a good idea." I wrapped my arm around his, silently ordering myself to relax with this man I adored. I struggled to get into the space that I knew he wanted me to be in.

Once we were on the gondola, Max wrapped his arm around my waist and pulled me close.

"I'm sorry I got frustrated earlier. I'm just trying to make this special, and maybe I'm pushing too much." He looked straight into my eyes. "Sammy, I meant it when I said that I value every moment we have together. Nothing about being with you is a sacrifice for me. Never think that, okay?"

"Okay." I smiled with gratitude. "But you don't need to apologize to me. I'm the one that's a little off, not you."

He gazed out over the water for a moment, then looked back at me. "I think that I don't always know the right thing to say to you, you know?"

"I know." I squeezed his hand. "You don't have to

worry about that, Max. I love you for who you are."

"I love you too, Sammy."

I rested my head against his shoulder. The lull of the boat rocking in the water, the subtle slash of the paddle, and the warmth of Max's chest joined together to tug me into slumber.

"Sammy?"

I forced my eyes open and looked up into Max's. "Max?"

"Are you okay?" He frowned.

"I'm sorry. Did I fall asleep?"

"Yes. The ride is over. We have to get onto the dock."

My heart sunk as I took his hand. He helped me onto the dock. He didn't say a word, but he didn't have to. I could see in the downturn of his lips that he wasn't pleased I'd missed the entire gondola ride.

"Maybe we should just head back to the hotel." He walked with me to the end of the dock. "I think it might be for the best."

"No way, I'm wide awake now. I promise." I kissed his cheek. "I'm ready to taste some gelato."

"You sure?" He studied me. "Sleep is important."

"I'm sure. I'm sorry I fell asleep on you. I won't let it happen again."

"Well, this is our first stop." He gestured to a small gelato shop not far from the dock. "The guide says that they're famous for a hazelnut flavor."

"Oh, yummy."

He held open the door for me.

CHAPTER 25

When we walked up to the counter an older man smiled at both of us.

"Welcome, welcome. What can I get for you?"

"We'd like a hazelnut gelato." Max placed the payment on the counter.

"Two?" He looked between us.

"No, just one." Max's smile was a little strained.

"And two spoons!" I nudged Max's elbow.

"Oh, you'll be back for more." The man grinned and handed Max the gelato and two spoons. "Enjoy."

Max and I stepped back outside. He held the cup out to me. "You get the first taste."

"Okay, I won't argue." I scooped up a tiny spoonful of the gelato. As the flavor melted onto my tongue I was so glad that I hadn't missed out on it. It was like nothing I'd ever tasted before—delicious and refreshing.

"Glad you liked it. Let's keep going." Max scooped big spoonfuls into his mouth as we walked.

I fixated on the dwindling gelato in the cup. I watched Max's spoon go from the cup to his lips. Just as he was about to take the last bite, I grabbed his arm.

"Max, look over there. Isn't it a beautiful boat?" I pointed to the water. As Max turned to look, I snatched the gelato right off of his spoon.

He turned back and nodded. "It's gorgeous." Then he looked at his spoon. "Funny, I thought I had one bite left."

I kept my lips sealed tight as the gelato melted in my mouth.

"Oh, well." He shrugged and threw the cup in a nearby garbage can. He held my hand as we walked through the narrow streets and took in the sights and sounds of Venice.

I took the map from Max's hand so that I could see what the next flavor would be. Lemon. *Oh, I do love anything lemon.* I sighed.

"Here it is." I pointed out the next shop to him.

Once more he ordered one gelato.

"First bite." He held the gelato out to me.

My eyes widened at the scent of it. I dipped the spoon in and this time took a larger spoonful. As soon as the spoon was in my mouth, Max began to devour what remained. I tried to savor the taste and ignore the fact that not getting more than that was upsetting me. It upset me so much that as Max went to scoop up his final bite, I pretended to bump into him. The cup jumped out of his hand and landed in my own.

"Oops! Sorry, Max."

"It's okay. Are you okay?"

"I'm fine. Oh, look, there's that boat again!" I pointed to the water.

He turned to look.

I licked the last bite right out of the gelato cup, then tossed the cup in the trash.

"Hey, I had a little left in there." He frowned.

"No, it was empty."

"Hm." He eyed me for a moment. "Okay, the next one isn't far up the road." He wrapped his arm around my shoulders and we walked together.

I tried to ignore the bit of guilt I felt for lying to him. It was gelato. Drastic measures were required. When we reached the next gelato shop he ordered one cup of strawberry. Once more he offered me the first bite. This time I swirled the spoon around until it was the biggest spoonful I could make.

"Oh, honey, that's a bit much. Want me to take some of that for you?" He swept his spoon in my spoon's direction.

"Back off, Max!" I stuck the spoonful in my mouth before he could get it.

He burst out laughing.

"Ah, I see that you are enjoying the gelato."

"Mmm." I sighed as the strawberry flavor melted on my tongue. By the time I opened my eyes, Max had eaten almost the entire cup.

He locked eyes with me as he swirled his spoon in the

last bit. "Do you want some more, Sammy?" He held the spoon up in the air near my lips.

"No. I said one spoonful of each. That's all." I shook my head.

He moved the spoon back and forth. I followed it with my eyes. He laughed again.

"Alright—going once, going twice." He opened his mouth.

I lunged forward and ate the last bite off of his spoon before it could reach his mouth. "I knew it!" He grinned at me. "You've been stealing my gelato, haven't you?"

"Maybe…" I savored the last bit of gelato.

"You had me thinking I was nuts. Want me to go get you another one?"

"No, thanks. I'm fine."

"If you say so. It's way past lunch. There's a pizza restaurant. Shall we give it a shot?"

"When in Italy…" I grinned.

CHAPTER 26

While Max ordered the pizza, I thought about the book signing the next day. Max requested that the day just be about us, but the pressure was still distracting me. I did feel that I was expected to perform and to look a certain way. I didn't want to disappoint the people who supported me. I nibbled on my slice of pizza and continued to think about it.

"Sammy, what's on your mind? Aren't you hungry? We've been walking all day."

"Oh, yes I am." I took a bite and sat back in my chair. "Oh, this is so good!" The pizza was better than any pizza I'd ever tasted.

Max continued to study me. "So what's up? What are you lost in thought about?"

"You said no business talk, remember?"

"Well, it doesn't really work if all you're doing is thinking about it." He smiled and took my hand. "It's okay. I always want to hear what's on your mind."

"I don't know, I guess I'm feeling a little stuck. Like I

can't quite figure out why, but this book signing tomorrow seems like the last thing I want to do."

"Really?" He lifted an eyebrow. "That's not like you."

"I know." I sighed and glanced at my watch.

"Why are you looking at your watch? Do you have an appointment today?"

"No. I guess I'm a little obsessed with keeping track of time right now."

"Hm, that's not like you either."

I met his eyes across the table. "You're right, it's not."

"Well, lately it has been." He tugged at my watchband. "It seems you're always checking the time."

"I never feel like there's enough time." I frowned. All of a sudden it made sense. "That's it, Max! That's what's wrong. I've been so worried about being at the right places at the right time that I've forgotten how to just be in the moment."

"That makes sense." He nodded. "We've been doing a lot of rushing and traveling." He hesitated and looked down at his slice of pizza.

"What is it, Max?"

"I don't want to fight." He looked across the table at me.

"I'm open to hearing what you have to say." I gave his hand a light pat.

"Well, to be honest, I was a little upset that you went to the meditation this morning."

"You were? Why?" I frowned.

"Because instead of getting the sleep you needed so that you could enjoy our day together, you pushed yourself again—to do something else. I know meditation is important to you, but it seems to me that if you'd let yourself sleep a little longer, you'd feel better for just getting the rest you need. It's like you're always afraid of missing out on something—but that fear is keeping you from experiencing anything fully." He shrugged. "I could be wrong. But I guess that's what was getting under my skin."

"Max, you know me so well. That's exactly what I was doing. From here on out, I'm in the moment." I smiled as I finished my slice of pizza. "And when we get to the next gelato stop, we're ordering two!"

"Good, that means no more stealing?" He wagged his finger at me playfully.

"I can't promise you that. But I'll try." I grinned.

We spent the rest of the day sharing moments—from stealing gelato from one another to taking one last ride on the gondola. When the stars came out above the city, I experienced it with Max's arm around me. It was a magical moment that might have been sacrificed if I hadn't taken the time to enjoy it.

When I woke up the next morning, my mind was filled with the memories of the day before. Although Max and I had talked it out, his words still impacted me. I wasn't taking the time to live. I wasn't participating in the things that mattered to me. I'd given in to the rush and pressure of pleasing others, all while leaving my own desires far behind. Sometimes that even seemed to include Max these days.

I looked over at him as he snored in his sleep. Even that was adorable. With a light touch I trailed my fingertips along his shoulder and down over his arm. I hadn't touched him so gently in quite some time. Max, my husband. The thought still made my body buzz with excitement. I snuggled closer to him and took the time to enjoy being near him.

After a few minutes my cell phone began to ring. I would have ignored it, but I didn't want it to wake Max. I grabbed it and saw that it was Isabella.

"Hello?" I slipped out of bed and walked into the living room.

"Hi, Samantha, I hope it's not too early. I just wanted to go over a few things with you."

"Sure."

"At the book signing we have time for a longer read. I'm hoping that you might be able to select a passage. If not, I can pick one out for you. I thought you would know better than me what would be best."

"Sure, I'll look through it." I sighed.

"Is something wrong?"

"I don't know exactly. I feel like I'm always reading to my fans. But they've already read my book, so why do they need to hear it again?"

"I think that some people just like to hear it in person. It's like seeing the author in action. Also, there may be people there that haven't read your book yet, and they will because of what they hear."

"I know, but doesn't it seem so routine to you?"

"I guess it's how we always do it."

"Would you be opposed to me getting a little creative at this book signing?"

"Like finger-paints creative or clothing optional creative?"

I laughed. "Don't worry, clothes will be required. I have an idea, but I have to make a few calls before I can know if it's a possibility. I'll call you back once I find out."

"Okay, that's fine, but the signing is at two, so make sure that you get back to me early enough so that I can plan."

"I will. I promise, Isabella."

CHAPTER 27

I hung up with Isabella, then dialed Daniella's number. With the phone tucked against my shoulder, I opened the small refrigerator and pulled out the ingredients I'd purchased the night before. As I waited for Daniella to answer I began to prepare Max's favorite omelette—eggs, cheese, bacon, and black olives. It wasn't the healthiest breakfast, but I knew it was something he'd enjoy waking up to.

"Hello? This is Daniella."

"Hi, Daniella, it's Samantha. You helped me with the dress for Alistair's show?"

"Oh yes, of course. I remember you, Samantha. I heard the show turned out great."

"Ah yes, the evening show did." I laughed a little. "Anyway, I wondered if you might be interested in helping me out with something."

"What is it?"

"Well, I'd like to do something a little different at my next book signing, which happens to be this afternoon. If it's too short notice, I understand. I'd like for you to bring some of your designs and let some of my fans put on a bit of a fashion show. What do you think?"

"That is very short notice. But it would be great publicity for me. What kind of models will you be using?"

"No certain kind. Just an assortment of shapes and sizes. I'd like to see if Sue would be willing to participate."

"I can give her a call for you. I don't know if she'll go for it, though."

"I hope she will. See what you can do."

"Absolutely. I think it's a great idea, Samantha. I'll call you back after I talk to Sue."

"Thanks, Daniella." I smiled and hung up the phone.

I flipped Max's omelette onto a plate and started to pick the plate up.

"Is that for me?" Max's voice drifted along right beside my ear. He'd crept up behind me while I was on the phone.

I jumped with surprise and the omelette went flying up into the air.

"Max!"

"I've got it, I've got it!" He grabbed the plate from me and ducked under the omelette. It landed with a splat on the plate. "See?" He lifted it up and grinned.

"You're lucky." I laughed. "Don't sneak up on people!"

"I don't sneak up on people—just you." He kissed the side of my neck. "Thank you for this. The smell woke me up. It's been awhile since I've had one."

"Enjoy it, Max. I want you to know how much I appreciate you. I'll get you some juice to go with it."

"I know, Sammy." He leaned in for a quick kiss before he released me.

As he settled at the table, I grabbed one of the blueberry muffins that were leftover. My cell phone rang before I could even sit down.

"Hi, Daniella, did you reach Sue?"

"Yes, I did, and she said she's willing to participate. I'll bring a wide range of sizes. I'm pretty excited!"

"Me too!" I smiled as I hung up the phone.

"What is it?" Max looked over at me. "I haven't seen that glow in your eyes in some time."

"I might have something up my sleeve." I grinned.

"Are you going to share?" He quirked an eyebrow.

"Only with you." I sat down across from him and shared my plan as we ate. By the time we'd finished, Max knew the whole plan. "So what do you think? Is it a mistake?"

"Absolutely not. It's you." He stroked my cheek. "And it's going to be great."

I leaned across the table and kissed him. "Good, because you're going to help me make a runway!"

"Sounds like fun. Exactly what we need. I'm so glad we had that time yesterday, Sammy. You know I support your career. I just want to make sure we don't lose sight of our relationship either."

"You support more than my career, Max. You

support me. I'm glad that you noticed what I went blind to. Not only did it allow us to reconnect, but it allowed me to reconnect with my creativity too." I looked into his eyes. "I know just how lucky I am to have you. You keep me focused."

"I'm lucky to have you too. I don't know how I got so lucky, but here we are. I couldn't think of another place I'd rather be."

"How about Amsterdam?" I grinned. "We leave tomorrow for the next leg of the tour."

"Wow! That's fast."

"Only if we let it be. We can take our time and not rush, then it won't seem so chaotic."

"Good plan." He leaned across the table and kissed me again. "Thanks for the omelette. I'll get changed and we can get to work on that runway."

I watched as Max walked back into the bedroom. No matter how many people I met along this crazy journey that was my life, Max remained the most beautiful man I'd ever seen.

It occurred to me then that he must see me that way too. No wonder it frustrated him when I put myself down. He thought I was as perfect as I thought he was.

When he returned, I stood up and hugged him. He started to pull away so we could leave, but I kept him in my arms. I hugged him until I could hear his heartbeat and sense the flow of his energy.

No matter how busy life got, I now knew that there

was no excuse for not taking the time to reconnect with him—or with myself.

CHAPTER 28

We arrived early at the venue for the book signing.
Max and I set about creating a curtained area for changing
and a small runway. I didn't want it to be intimidating. I
didn't want anyone to worry about falling. I just wanted
every woman who set foot on the runway to be proud.

Soon my other models arrived, as did Daniella with a
wide range of garments. As the women sorted out what
they wanted to wear, I noticed Isabella walking toward
me. I braced myself for her reaction. Would she shut the
whole idea down?

"Samantha, there's a woman at the front door
without a ticket. She said that you invited her?" Isabella
looked over the curtain and runway. "It looks good."

"A woman?" I shook my head. "I'm not sure who she
is. Let me go see."

When I reached the front door I was still puzzled.

"Hello, I'm Samantha."

"Hi, I'm Amelia. My husband met you at the train
station the other night. He's a security guard there. He
said that you'd told him that if I wanted to attend one of

your book signings, I could. If that's not okay, I can leave." She lowered her eyes.

I smiled at her. Amelia had what I considered to be a heart-shaped body. She was short in stature with bowed-out hips and a rounded stomach. Her legs were thin, as were her arms and her chest was full. She was beautiful and exactly what I needed.

"It's not a problem at all. In fact you're exactly who I need. Would you be willing to take part in a fashion show?"

When I saw the fear in her eyes, I was sure that it was the same fear that had been seen in my own eyes when I was asked to walk the runway for Alistair.

"I don't know if I could do that." She shook her head. "Why would you want me to?"

"Because you're gorgeous, and I want to show you off." I grinned. "It's just for our little book signing—no cameras, no huge audience. What do you say?"

"Okay. I guess if you think I'd be able to do it." She shrugged.

"Wonderful." I walked her back to the other women and Daniella. "I have our last model, Daniella."

"Wow! Perfect!" Daniella snatched up a dress and held up to Amelia. "This will look stunning on you."

I stood back as the women gathered together and tried on different outfits until each found the one that she was most comfortable in. It surprised me that once they got over the hurdle of discomfort, they giggled and chatted just like little girls. It reinforced the belief in my mind that every woman, no matter how she protested, wanted the opportunity to feel beautiful.

Sue selected a billowy dress. I wanted to let her make her own choice, but I was drawn to question her about it.

"Sue, with your figure, this one might be better." I held up a sleek dress that I thought would fit her perfectly.

"Maybe." She hesitated. "But this one has a bit more room in the skirt."

"Sue." I bit into my bottom lip. I didn't want to cross a line and offend her, but I wanted her to have the opportunity to be proud of her body. "Is it because you want to tuck away your hand?"

"Yes." Sue frowned. "I'm just more comfortable that way."

I took her hand in mine and trailed my fingertips across it. "Your hand is beautiful, just like you are. Why would you be more comfortable hiding it? Don't you think that you're hiding a part of yourself by doing that?"

"Maybe." She looked down at her hand in mine. "It's never going to be perfect."

"It's already perfect." I smiled at her. "There's no reason to hide it. It is part of you, it is formed of you, and you are beautiful. Don't let what other people might say or think stop you from finding pride in every inch of your body. I'm sure that if you were allowed to look deep enough, you'd find some things that they are trying to hide too."

"Yes, probably." She laughed a little. "When I was teased as a little girl, I always thought to myself—well, you might have two whole hands, but that doesn't change the ugly inside."

"You're right. It's your choice. If you really feel more comfortable hiding your hand, I won't do a thing to stop you, but I wonder if that little girl inside of you would really want you to do that." I smiled at her as her eyes widened.

"I guess I didn't really think of it that way. Maybe I'll try the other dress." She looked it over with a hint of envy. "I've always wanted to wear something so sleek and tight. I always wondered how I'd look in it."

"Try it on, and if you like it, wear it for the show." I gave her a quick hug.

As the women finished getting dressed I walked up to Daniella. "Thanks for doing all this on such short notice."

"Of course. When you called me, I was really excited." She brushed a dress bag back along the rack. "I think it's a wonderful idea."

"Good. Then maybe you won't mind me asking you to take part." I looked into her eyes.

CHAPTER 29

Daniella shook her head and smiled. "Oh no, remember, I told you I'm not the type of person to do that."

"Daniella, there are no flashing cameras here." I paused a moment and looked at the garment bag. "You can't tell me that while designing clothes for all kinds of women, you didn't design something special just for yourself."

Daniella glanced over at the bag as well. "Maybe I did." She shrugged. "But that doesn't mean that I want to be part of some kind of fashion show."

"I'm not asking you to be part of a fashion show. I'm asking you to walk with pride. I'm asking you to put on display your passion for your work—to bring one of your dresses to life."

"You are quite persuasive, you know." She looked over at me and grinned. "I guess it couldn't hurt."

"No one is going to fall! I promise!"

"And no wardrobe malfunctions." She laughed.

"I hope not." I grinned.

"Alright, I'll do it. Why not?" She unzipped the garment bag and revealed a brilliant blue evening dress.

I'd never seen anything like it. It was intertwined with tulle and tiny gold stars that were only noticeable when the light shined on it.

"Samantha?" Isabella poked her head inside. "Is everything going okay in here?"

"Yes, it's fine."

"Good, because I need you out front. There's someone here to see you." She smiled.

"Oh?" I stepped out from behind the curtain and noticed that all of the seats were filled for the book signing. To my surprise Alistair stood beside the book signing table.

"Samantha, I just need a moment of your time."

"Sure, Alistair. What is it?" I paused beside the table.

"I heard that you were putting on your very own fashion show. I guess that I had quite an influence on you." His smile spread into a grin.

"You could say that." I nodded and glanced toward the curtain. "Daniella is helping me with it."

"Daniella?"

"Your seamstress?" I raised an eyebrow. "She did the alterations on my dress."

"Oh. I don't think we've ever met. She does very good work, though."

"She is a designer too. You should stick around for

the show. There's still a seat available up front." I pointed to an empty chair near the table.

"Maybe I will. I thought I'd just congratulate you on having your own show, but it sounds interesting."

"It's just for fun. I thought it would be a nice way for a few women to show their pride in their bodies. In fact, another one of your employees is in it too."

"Another? Should I be concerned that you're stealing all my people?" He raised an eyebrow. "What's next? My firstborn?"

I laughed. "No, I think you're safe there. Just sit back and enjoy."

"Alright, I will." He walked over to the empty chair.

My heart skipped a beat. It was one thing to put on a little show for a room full of fans; it was another thing to have a well-known designer sitting in the front row. I wondered for a moment if I should tell the others about Alistair's presence.

In the end, I decided against it. I didn't want anyone to get too nervous.

Isabella signaled to me that the session was about to start. I stepped up to the podium and smiled at the audience before me.

"Thank you, everyone, for being here today. Your support is something I can never thank you enough for. I know that normally we do a brief reading from the book, but I'm fairly certain most of you have read it already. Am I right?"

Most of the people in the audience nodded in agreement.

"So instead of doing that today, I wanted to try something a little different. Ever since I started this tour, I've been provided with some amazing opportunities. Some of those experiences have been a little challenging for me, which I now realize I needed. That comfort zone always needs to be stretched.

"But something else I discovered is that even when great things happen, even when everything is going just the way you want it to, it's very easy to lose sight of yourself. It is so important to slow down and refocus, to get to know yourself again.

"I really had an adventure at the last book signing. I had the chance to wear a beautiful dress and take part in a fashion show presented by a talented designer. As grateful as I was for the experience, I had a hard time feeling comfortable. I couldn't figure it out. Then I realized that it was because I wasn't following my passion.

"These book signings, the book itself—it's not about image. It's about inspiring women all over the world to be who they truly are. The truth is, I was not being who I truly was.

"In place of a reading, we're going to have our own fashion show. The designs were created by a woman—for women of all shapes and sizes. It may be a little unconventional, but I think that Zara would approve."

As I stepped back from the podium the room filled

with applause.

CHAPTER 30

As each woman stepped through the curtain, I could see the pride in their eyes and the shine of their smiles. They weren't trying to sell anything. They were just being themselves, as happily and proudly as they could be. All of the garments fit perfectly, not just for their shape, but for their personality.

When Sue stepped out, my breath caught in my throat. Not only had she decided to wear the fitted dress, she'd accented her arm right down to her fingertips with a thin satin ribbon. She'd chosen to draw attention to a part of her that she'd been hiding for so long. It brought tears to my eyes to think that she was brave enough to give herself that moment of freedom.

Alistair sat forward at the sight of her. I noticed his eyes widen. He pulled out his phone and snapped a picture.

Daniella was the final woman to walk the runway. Her dress caught every light in the room and gave her a subtle glow that was reflected in the brilliance of her smile. As she reached the end of the runway, I looked over at Alistair. This time he wasn't shy about taking a picture. He took several.

As the fashion show ended I stepped back up to the podium.

"I'd like to invite any of you that would like to take the same walk up here to try it out. There's an assortment of clothing to try if you'd like, or just stay in what you're wearing. As beautiful as the clothes are, it isn't about the clothes. It's about the confidence. It's about seeing yourself as the beautiful person that you are."

A few of the audience members stood up to join in. I started to walk over to them, but Alistair grabbed me by the arm.

"That last woman on the runway—who was that?"

"That was Daniella, your seamstress. Isn't she amazing?"

"She's the one who designed all of these garments?" He looked toward the curtain.

"Yes, she is." I smiled as I followed his line of sight. "She's really talented."

"She's more than that. I'm going to have to get her on my team before she puts me out of business." He grinned. "And I had no idea that Sue had such a beautiful presence on the runway. Thank you for bringing them to my attention."

"I'm sure they'd both love to hear that from you." I gestured to the women as they began to file out from behind the curtain.

"I will do just that."

As he walked away, that warmth, that sense of peace that I'd experienced for a brief moment during meditation, finally returned to me. I didn't need to be anything more than who I was. My instincts always seemed to steer me in the right direction.

Max walked up to me with a bouquet of flowers. "Sammy, that was quite a surprise. You amaze me every day." He leaned in for a kiss, then started to pull back right away.

I tangled my fingers in his hair and drew him back for a longer kiss. Then I looked into his eyes. "I'm done rushing through things and trying to prove myself. I'm ready to savor the time we're sharing, whether we're in Italy or back home."

"Great." He took my hands in his. "Because I want to do the same."

Isabella walked up to me with a wide smile. "This was fantastic, Samantha. I'm so glad you chose to do this here. Listen, I went ahead and forwarded your number to your contact in Amsterdam. There's been a bit of a shuffling of people there, so I don't personally know your contact, but I'm sure it will all be fine."

I raised an eyebrow. "If you're so sure, then why do you look so worried?"

"If you have any trouble, just call me." She patted my hand. "Enjoy your last night in Venice."

"Thank you for everything, Isabella."

When she walked away I looked at Max. "That was a little strange, don't you think?"

"Don't worry about it, I'm sure it'll be fine—just like she said."

As we left the venue my cell phone rang. I didn't recognize the number.

"Hello?"

"Hallo! This is Erik!" The jovial voice in my ear made it sound like he was shouting.

"Erik? I'm sorry, I'm not sure if you have the right number."

"Samantha?"

"Yes, this is Samantha."

"Then I have the right number. I'm looking forward to meeting you in Amsterdam tomorrow."

"There must be some kind of mix-up. Usually my contacts are women."

"No mix-up. I can wear a skirt if you like." He laughed loudly.

I looked over at Max and raised an eyebrow. "No, that's fine. I'm looking forward to meeting you too, Erik."

"Wonderful. See you tomorrow." He hung up before I could respond.

"Who was that?" Max laughed. "I could hear him laughing."

"He's my contact for Amsterdam. Erik."

"Erin?"

"No, Erik. It's a guy."

"Huh. I thought it was going to be all women?" He shrugged. "I guess this should be interesting."

"Very." I bit into my bottom lip.

Live in the moment, Sammy, live in the moment. I tried, but I couldn't help but wonder exactly how I was going to get along with the boisterous Erik in Amsterdam.

I took a deep breath and cleared my mind. I was still in Venice, with the love of my life, and I was going to make the last few hours count.

"Uh, Max?"

"Yes?" He looked over at me.

"Are you thinking what I'm thinking?" I gazed into his eyes.

"I think I might be." He drew me close to him and returned my heated stare. "In fact, I know I am."

I leaned close and kissed him. He returned the kiss.

The moment we broke apart, we spoke at the same time.

"Gelato!"

"Yes!" I laughed. "There's always time for gelato."

A NOTE FROM THE AUTHOR

Fictional character, Samantha Bradford and the Single Wide Female books are written for every woman out there who has struggled with their weight, self-esteem and any number of issues that we all face as we work to become the best versions of ourselves that we can be.

These books are meant to be light-hearted and fun, with the hope that they will also inspire you to make your own "bucket list" of sorts—and to REALLY live your life to the fullest, loving yourself completely as you do so.

Lillianna loves to hear from her readers and can be contacted via her website where you can also download a complimentary book.

LilliannaBlake.com

ALL TITLES BY LILLIANNA BLAKE

http://Amazon.com/author/lilliannablake
*Check the author page for current list of titles

Single Wide Female: The Bucket List

#1 Learn Pole Dancing

#2 Start a Blog

#3 Learn to Cook

#4 Create a Masterpiece

#5 Run a Marathon

#6 Go Skinny Dipping

#7 Start Online Dating

#8 Learn Yoga

#9 Be a Mentor

#10 Crash a Wedding

#11 Be a Movie Extra

#12 Join a Writing Group

#13 Enjoy a Spa Day

#14 Donate Blood

#15 Learn Poker

#16 Get a Tattoo

#17 Host a Dinner Party

#18 Publish a Book

#19 Walk Across Hot Coals

#20 Learn to Swim

#21 Learn to Meditate

#22 Quit My Job

#23 Learn to Salsa

#24 Fall in Love

Visit the author website at LilliannaBlake.com to get on the notification list for new releases and to receive a complimentary book to learn what inspired Sammy to begin her bucket list.